SILVERBACK

SIMON MINCHIN

CLIMBING TREE BOOKS

First published 2019 by Climbing Tree Books Ltd.

Copyright © Simon Minchin 2019

ISBN: 978-1-909172-48-7

Published by Climbing Tree Books Ltd, Truro, Cornwall

www.climbingtreebooks.com

www.simonminchin.com

Cover photo by the author

Author portrait by Lee Searle

Cover design by Ryan Mcfarlane and Grace Kennard

Typeset by Grace Kennard

I'd like to dedicate this book to you. I hope you enjoy it.
I'd like to thank Sergio, for getting me started on this journey,
and William for showing me the path to walk.
Love to Claire, Beanie and Arri. Love to all xx xx

Simon Minchin

CONTENTS

HIGHTIDE

HE WAS an old man who sailed alone on a catamaran and he had gone twenty-eight days now without touching land.

He kept his head close-shaved but his silver and grey beard grew thick and bushy, apart from the side of his jaw where it would never grow again. He spent most of his time naked and the sun and salt had tanned his skin to a tough, resilient hide. His shoulders and arms were bulky from grinding the winches that raised the boat's sails. His legs seemed to come from another body, almost another creature. The Marlin was only thirty-five feet long and for the last ten years it was a rare day when he had walked any further than that.

If the old man looked like a testimony to how he had lived for the last decade, then his boat reflected those years doubly so.

The Marlin had started life as a rich man's bauble, a Wildcat 35 that had first gone into the sea in Florida. Now she was over four thousand miles to the northeast and looking more like an Everglades hillbilly than a Miami Beach lawyer. The sails were patches on patches and the twin hulls were hidden beneath a thick layer of plastic water barrels, battered flight cases and bulging cargo nets. There was barely an inch of the boat that didn't have something tied to it; she looked like a five-ton rubbish heap under sail, but all that rubbish was invaluable. In the cockpit, facing the wheel, the old man had bolted down a salt-rimmed brown leather armchair; an ex-military tarpaulin was stretched over the top for shade. The Marlin towed a fiberglass dinghy on a short length of rope and a floating necklace of water barrels on a longer one.

She was a speck of dirt floating in a crystal-clear and sparkling sea. She was the old man's life and, usually, his entire world.

'Hello, what's that then?' said the old man, squinting at something on the horizon.

The Marlin didn't answer him. She never did.

The old man listened for her though. He heard small waves slapping at the hulls, he heard the rigging playing the mast like an over-sized tubular bell. He heard the utter silence as a seagull floated overhead and he heard the thousand tiny creaks and squeaks as the Marlin and her disorderly cargo moved on the surface of the calm sea.

'It's land, isn't it?' he said. 'Oh, bollocks.'

.

Friday ran towards the shore.

She thought the grass beneath her bare feet felt as smooth and soft as a kitten's fur and the sun seemed like a warm, loving arm hugging her shoulders.

That made her happy.

She was supposed to be looking for stuff that had

washed up on the shoreline, that's what the others had sent her out to do but hardly anything was washed up these days. A few years ago, when she had first been given this as her job, she would find all sorts of things at the high tide mark but now her hunt for beached treasure was more an excuse to get away from the others and be on her own.

Friday was twelve. Twelve was quite grown up but not so grown up that she wanted to spend much time with the adults and most of the other children were such babies.

At the point where the grass ended and the land slumped down towards the beach in an untidy, gravel and stone cliff, Friday stopped. This was one of her favourite places for finding treasure. Below the cliff and going out into the sea was a tangle of stumps, broken trees and roots. It was a forest that the sea had washed again and again until it had washed every last leaf and every single stick away. It was a forest that was part way under water, a forest where only the big bits were left. The waves had pounded and rinsed the wood until it was as smooth and polished as stone. It was a perfect place to explore, an ideal spot to find stuff caught in the jumbled-up trees, a lovely place just to lie on one of the bigger fallen trunks and bathe in the sun.

Friday scrambled down the cliff and out onto the drowning deadfall. At first there was mud and silt glistening slickly beneath the trunks and branches but as she moved further out little waves came lapping beneath her and, when she was as far out as she could go, it was as if she was out at sea riding the world's most badly made raft.

Friday wasn't scared of the sea, not like some of the others. Some of the older grown-ups had nightmares about it, but for her it was something that had always been in her life. The sea surrounded the island she lived on and it separated her island from the others that were out towards the horizon. The sea was like a cliff or a tunnel or one of the ruins or a cave or…anything really. If you were sensible and played nicely, it wouldn't hurt you.

Friday tugged her rag of a dress off over her head and bundled it up to use as a pillow. The material was so threadbare that it was hardly much softer than the tree beneath. She closed her eyes and sprawled and stretched feeling just like the big, old ginger cat that lived in the village. When she opened her eyes, she was looking straight up into the blue sky and the clouds that floated in it.

That one like a dragon. There was almost always a dragon.

That one like a bird.

That one was going to be a rat but the wind must have changed because she watched it turn into a fish.

She stretched again and this time a splinter of wood jabbed at the round, brown stone of her bottom.

'Ow,' said Friday, and sat up.

She pulled the salt-caked blonde curls of her hair back from her face and looked around. The circlet of islands was such a familiar sight to her and it was so rare that the view changed at all that she spotted the boat almost immediately. Out there, out there past the GodStone was a sail and a sail always meant a boat and a boat always meant new people and new things; everyone knew that.

'One for the master, and one for the dame, and one for the little girl who lives down the lane,' sang Friday happily to herself but she sang it in her own head because there was no one around to hear her.

After that first faint purple-grey smudge on the horizon had slowly revealed itself to be not one, but at least two or three islands, the old man had set the self-steering gear on a course towards them.

There was just the lightest breeze. He would have plenty of time to think before he got there.

Twenty-eight days was a fair old time between landfalls and he could do with filling up the main water tank, perhaps trading some fish for a little meat. The old man was in no great hurry to see people again, but it needn't be for long and most folk were pretty peaceful these days. The ones who were wrapped a little too tight just simply didn't seem to last long.

'What do you reckon, old girl?' he said to the Marlin. 'Shall we go and have a look?' Taking silence for agreement, the old man shook out another metre or two of sail and the boat picked up a little speed. He scrambled over the top of the cockpit and then slid down the slope of the cabin to land on the trampoline between the two hulls at the bow. Stretching out his skinny legs, he idly scratched at his balls.

The Marlin made a soothing schlop...schlop...schlop as the hulls cut through the waves. The rigging rattled from time to time but other than that, the world was so quiet that the old man could hear his own breathing, the tide of air running in and out of his lungs. He scratched at the big patch of scar tissue that knotted his chest. More than ten years and it still itched. How did that even make sense?

As the boat drew closer to the archipelago, he could see that there were five larger islands and another handful of lumps, bumps and rocks in a bracelet around a central bay and that there was something slap-bang in the middle of the bay. The Marlin slipped between the first two islands and into the circle. There were no signs of life but that didn't mean that life wasn't there.

He scrambled back over the cockpit and took the wheel. Reefed the sails a little and the Marlin slowed to a creep then a little less and she came to a stop right next to the object sticking up from the sea. It was covered in barnacles and splattered with seagull shit but the old man knew what it was even before he looked down through the clear water at what lay hidden beneath. Curtained in a thick yellow weave of kelp it disappeared down and down into the depths as far as he could see.

'Well I fuckin' never,' said the old man to himself.

He was about to explore when, in the corner of his eye, he saw movement. There was a figure standing on the beach of one of the islands waving at him, a tiny brown figure with blonde hair.

.

'Hello, hello, hello, hello, hellooow, hello, hello,' sang Friday as she danced and waved her arms above her head. After a minute she could tell that the people on the boat had seen her because the sail came up a bit more and the boat turned until it was pointed right at her. That was good, they were coming to say hello. Perhaps she should show them where it was safe to land? Friday scrambled back along the mess of trunks and branches until she was standing on the muddy beach once again. She walked off to the left a little way until she reached a place where there were no rocks or trees or anything else that a boat might bump into. She waved her hands again and then pointed to the bit of beach she was standing on. That should do it.

Friday sat down and began to poke at the mud with a stick to see what she might find.

A bit later she looked out into the bay again. The sun had dropped closer to the horizon and the sunlight was bouncing across the sea like diamonds skimmed on water. The sky had picked up that slight haze that told Friday it was going to be a perfect, still and sunny evening. The world was beautiful.

It seemed that the boat had come to a stop. Now she could see it more closely, it looked like two boats tied together. That was funny. And there was a man climbing into a little rowing boat and paddling towards her. Perhaps she was just going to meet just one new person after all. Well, that would be good too.

.

The old man beached the dinghy and stepped on to dry-ish land for the first time in a month. The mud squeezed up between his toes and his feet slid in the fine silt of the beach.

'Hello,' he said and stuck his hand out. 'My name's Ernest, but you can call me Ernie.'

Friday looked suspiciously at his hand. It looked funny. 'Where are your other fingers?' she asked.

Ernie smiled rather sadly. 'I lost them,' he said. 'Well, someone took them from me actually. But it was a long time ago. It doesn't hurt, but you can shake this hand if you want,' and he stuck out his left.

Friday thought for a moment. 'No. It's OK. I'll shake your poorly hand,' and she took hold of his two remaining fingers and squeezed them. 'I'm Friday,' she said and frowned when the old man laughed.

He saw her face and bit his lip in penance. 'No, don't. I'm sorry,' he said. 'That was rude, but there's a story about a person who lands on an island and meets someone called Friday, but that's a "Man Friday". I'm sorry. "Friday" is a nice name.'

Friday thought about this and then smiled up at him.

'Fingers are important,' said Friday. 'Your fingers are all different sizes so that they fit into the different bits in your body. You know, like in your ears and up your nose and that. It's like a toolkit,' and she demonstrated by picking some snot out of her nose. 'It must be horrid to be missing some.'

'It was a long time ago,' said Ernie. 'Don't you want to put your dress on?' When Ernie had seen that it was a little girl waiting for him on the shore he had pulled on a pair of shorts but Friday stood in front of him brown and naked and holding her scrumpled-up dress in one hand.

'I'm not cold,' she said.

Ernie smiled. 'Come, let's go and sit on the grass and you can tell me your story.'

'I don't have a story,' said Friday.

'Sure you do. We all do. It just means, tell me about who you are and what you do and how you came to be here.'

'Because the GodStone chose me,' said Friday. 'That's why we're all here, because the GodStone chose us to live.'

Ernie sucked at his teeth and chewed his lip. He led Friday up the gentle slope to where the grass began and they both sat down looking out over the bay. Friday got up, spread her dress on the grass beneath her and sat down again. 'Tickles,' she said to Ernie by way of explanation.

'So..?' said Ernie.

Friday looked at him. 'Oh, you mean my story. Tell you my story.'

Ernie nodded.

'Me and the others live in the village on the other side of the island. We were all chosen by the GodStone and that's why we have a dry place to live on and why we aren't drowned. God drowned all the bad people and sometimes He sends us a bad person to skarifice so that He knows we remember to be good.'

Ernie took a deep, deep breath. 'When did the god drown the bad people?' he asked.

'Just before I was born. I'm one of the first new, shining-bright ones. Well, that's what The Father says.'

'How old are you?'

Friday took one of her blonde curls, pulled it to her mouth and sucked the salt from it. 'Do you want to see my village?' she asked.

Ernie thought about this for a little while. 'Who's "The Father"?'

'He looks after us and tells us what to do so that the drowning doesn't come back and he does the skarificing to keep the GodStone happy. He can be quite strict and we have to do what he says. You know, like a proper father.'

'God didn't drown the world,' said Ernie very quietly.

Friday looked cross. 'The Father says that the world was full of bad people and God made the sea come onto the land and drown them all apart from some good ones that He saved. And He put the GodStone there to remind us.' She pointed out into the bay. 'You've seen the GodStone. I saw you stop there.'

'Yeah,' said Ernie. 'I stopped there. How many people

are in your village?'

Friday frowned and nodded her head from side to side. Ernie could tell that she was counting in her head.

'More than a hundred?' he asked.

'What's "a hunred"?' she replied. 'There's me and Bessie and Jack and Evie and…'

'Not that many then,' said Ernie. 'Just a little village, eh.'

'It is now,' said Friday. 'And it's getting littler.' She frowned and stabbed at the grass with a stick.

They sat quietly for a little while. Each one of them had learnt something new but neither was quite sure what it was yet.

'What happened to your face?' asked Friday.

Ernie touched the hard whorls of scar tissue. 'I was burnt,' he said.

'When you lost your fingers?' she asked and Ernie nodded.

Suddenly he turned and looked at Friday. 'Is this what the Father does?' He pointed at the burn scars. 'Is this scarification? Does he mark people like this?'

Friday winced. 'No,' she said with a frown. 'He does skarificing. Sometimes a new person comes to be skarified. You know, someone like you, and sometimes it has to be someone from the village mostly because they have done something bad or made The Father cross or something. The Father makes them stand in the sea and the sea goes higher and higher up their bodies until it covers their heads and they drown. But they drown so that the rest of us don't have to and every time, after the sea has gone over the person's head, it goes back down again rather than keeping on rising and drowning us all.' Friday nodded with the truth of it. 'So, The Father must be right, mustn't he? The sea drowns that one person instead of all of us.'

'Why doesn't the person run away or swim off?' asked Ernie.

'Because we break their ankles first with stones and then we weigh their feet down with rocks and their hands are tied to a post.'

'And then you drown them,' said Ernie quietly.

'No,' said Friday. 'The sea drowns them.'

Ernie sighed and chewed at the ball of his thumb. 'You mean "sacrifice" don't you? Not "skarifice". You sacrifice them.'

'Skarifice,' said Friday proudly. 'Yes. That's what I said.'

For a time they were both silent and watched the seagulls dance patterns in the sky; they watched as quietly as if they were the audience at a ballet.

.

'I'm leaving,' said Ernie eventually. 'I'm not going to visit your village. But I'll take you out to see the GodStone if you want. But put your dress on, it's colder out on the sea.'

Friday thought for a moment. 'And then you'll bring me back?' she asked. 'If you still want me to,' said Ernie.

Together they pushed the dinghy off the silt and when it was floating freely in the water Ernie picked Friday up and dropped her down onto the seat at the stern. He stepped up onto the bench in the middle and pulled himself aboard then, using one of the oars to push, he turned the boat around and when she was pointed out to sea, he slid the oars into the rowlocks and bent his back to row.

Friday caught sight of something under the seat and

pointed at it. 'What's that?' she asked. Ernie glanced down at the Remington shotgun. 'That's a "Just in Case"', he said. 'But I don't think I'll need it today.'

He rowed for a little while. Friday watched him.

Eventually he said, 'God didn't drown the world you know, men did.'

'The Father says...' But Ernie shook his head and shushed her. 'I've heard a bit of your story,' he said. 'Now listen to mine.'

The oar-blades sliced into the crystal-clear waters as Ernie rowed. The brass-bound wooden blades dripped pearls of saltwater back to the sea on each backstroke. The rowlocks creaked and the bow was slapped by petulant wavelets as the dinghy slipped towards the GodStone.

'God didn't drown the world, men did.'

Friday frowned but sat quietly.

'Something like, what, twenty years ago? Perhaps twenty-five, it's hard to keep track, there was an awful lot more people and an awful lot more land. Then there was a thing called "global warming". It sounds nice, doesn't it?' Friday nodded. 'Perhaps if we'd called it something more frightening people would have taken a bit more notice. But we didn't.'

'Who is "we"?' asked Friday. 'Were you in charge?'

Ernie laughed, a clear, happy laugh like the sound of sunshine. 'No,' he said. 'Not me. I don't know that anybody was. We all blamed the super-rich and the greedy. We blamed industry and governments and the big corporations and then, when the sea began to rise and drown the land, we blamed each other. But we'd all done our bit to make it happen. We were all to blame. Every last one of us.'

'Not God then?' said Friday. 'Did you light too many

fires? Was it all the fires that made the world get hot?'

'In a way. We filled the air with smoke and gas and pollution and that changed the sky; it changed the air, and the world got warmer.'

'Why didn't you stop? If you knew what you were doing why didn't you stop?'

'We were fools.'

'Everybody?' asked Friday. 'All the people in the whole wide world? Everybody was stupid?' She shook her head. 'I think The Father's story makes more sense.'

Ernie chuckled. 'Yeah,' he said. 'When you hear it said out loud, I know what you mean.' He stopped rowing and chewed on the ball of his thumb again. 'The ice melted, the sea rose and when it started to drown people we began to fight each other for what land was left.'

'Was that when...' Friday pointed at Ernie's scars.

He nodded. 'I lost these two fingers and someone burned me with petrol here on my chest and down the side of my face, here where there's no beard anymore. I killed them.' Ernie hugged himself. 'Then they killed my wife and my daughter.' He stared off into the sun. 'Then I killed more of them, a lot more. Then I found this boat and...'

'We're nearly there,' said Friday and sure enough the GodStone was just a few meters away. Ernie shipped the oars and they floated next to the barnacle-covered obelisk. He fished around in the bow locker and pulled out a snorkel and mask. 'Can you swim?' he asked Friday.

'Of course,' she said. 'But I don't know what those things are.'

He showed her how to put the mask on. 'We won't bother with this,' he said and put the snorkel aside then, first Ernie and then Friday rolled out of the dinghy into the sea and began treading water. 'Come on, follow me,' said Ernie and he duck-dived beneath the surface.

.

Twenty minutes later, exhausted by dive after dive, they pulled themselves back into the dinghy. The pair of them lay across the wooden seats like seals basking in the evening sun. Beads of salt water decorated their brown bodies until, imperceptibly slowly, they evaporated away. At last, warm and dry, they lay there, blinking at each other.

'It's a cathedral,' said Ernie. 'A drowned cathedral. Your GodStone is, or used to be, a house of god.'

'It's beautiful,' said Friday.

'Yeah, it is,' said Ernie. 'The bit sticking out of the water is just the very top of the spire. The cross must have fallen off long ago.'

'It looks like angels made it. What you can see under the water, all those towers and spikes and arches and windows, they look so beautiful. Only angels or fairies could make that.

Ernie sat still and quiet. Then he said, 'We weren't angels, we were monsters.'

Friday reached out and took Ernie's hand and squeezed it.

'Tell me again,' she said.

Ernie blew some snot from his nose then sat up straight and smiled at Friday, her straggled and soaked blonde curls, her thin brown body and her wide-eyed innocence. 'We drowned the world,' he said. 'We thought it would take years; hundreds of years and there would be time to fix it, somehow. Or at least that it wouldn't be our problem.

We would all be dead and gone and someone else…'

'Your children,' said Friday.

'Yes. Our children or their children would sort it out but something changed and it all happened much more quickly. Both the ice caps melted completely in just ten years and the sea level rose by almost eighty metres. And there was no time. There was no plan. Just fear and fighting and then… then this.'

Friday seemed to think about this for a long time. She drew shapes with her finger in the water that had splashed on to the bench seat. She tasted the salt on her finger. 'I don't believe you,' she said. 'It makes more sense that God drowned the world because the people were bad than the people drowned their own world because they were stupid and selfish.'

'It does,' said Ernie. 'But it isn't true.'

He slipped the oars back into the rowlocks and dipped them into the sea. 'Come on,' he said. 'We'd better go. I can take you back to the island or you can come with me on the Marlin and I'll show you things that will make you believe me. What do you think?'

Friday lent back on the dinghy seat and a truant smile settled on her face. 'I never really liked The Father much anyway,' she said. 'I think I'd like to come with you.'

SUSTAINABLE HEAT

THESE ARE things that you should know about Barnaby Abbott. He believes in God and he's as tight-fisted as the very devil. Barnaby is 87 and has the face of a wax death mask left near a warm fire.

Barnaby likes to be called 'Barnaby'. He doesn't like being called, 'Sir' and if you were to call him 'Barny' he wouldn't respond. That isn't to say that he wouldn't answer to 'Barny', that is to say that he would never, ever speak to you again. The people who have called Barnaby 'Barny' have ceased to exist by his reckoning. Utterly. Barnaby Abbott is a man of principle and a principle isn't a principle until it has cost you something. Barnaby's principles have cost him almost every relationship he has ever had, close or distant, family, friend or foe. Most of the people Barnaby has ever met have found some way to piss him off and also it must be said, he them.

Barnaby is prickly.

Having said that, if you can find merit in phrases like, 'he tells it like it is' and 'what you see is what you get', then you might be someone who can find something to like in

Barnaby. Jack Harrington can't stand those phrases and he's none too fond of the people who spout them but Jack took a shine to Barnaby the first time they met and for some reason that neither can really figure out, the relationship seems to have stood the test of time.

Jack is Barnaby's gardener. That is to say that he visits once a week and does whatever jobs Barnaby can find that need doing and are outside the house. Cut the grass. Weed the borders. Trim the hedges. Dig the drains. Chop the firewood.

Jack has been visiting Barnaby for a good few years now and over time the jobs have changed a little. Cutting the grass used to be a labour of love and was one that both men took some pride in. Jack used to weed and feed the lawns. He used to bring an old power-rake once a year and scratch all the moss and dead thatch out of the grass. Barnaby and Jack used to have long discussions about the exact length to cut the grass at any particular point during the season and, as often as not, would stop and admire the rolling green sward that they felt, quite rightly, they had produced together. It was one of those 'vanity lawns' that only the English can get quite so anal about.

Then one day Barnaby got a dog.

The dog would be a companion now that Barnaby's wife was in the care home. The dog would need walking and help Barnaby take the exercise he no longer took. The dog would be a friend to Barnaby now that his list of human friends was pretty much exhausted.

This turned out to be, not entirely the case.

The dog was a puppy and Barnaby was no spring chicken. The dog took to bullying Barnaby, to demanding walks that Barnaby didn't have the energy to give and to leaping up in an affectionate way that on more than one occasion put the pensioner flat on his back.

Barnaby locked the dog outside where it tried to burn off its energy and frustration by running around and around the lawn until it had worn itself a wide and muddy oval racetrack. The rest of the grass it covered in coiled lengths of dog shit and patches of pissed-on, yellowed turf.

Barnaby found the dog a new owner with stronger legs and a firmer hand but by that time the love affair with the lawn was over.

The borders still needed weeding though.

When Jack had first started with the Abbotts, Barnaby's wife still lived at home. She was beginning to suffer from dementia, but she still liked to sit in her chair looking out over the garden and took some pleasure from the blooms in the beds and borders. Yellow was her favourite colour and Barnaby, by instructing Jack, made sure that her view was as full of sunflowers and daffs, chrysanthemum and dahlia.

When Mrs Abbott became a little too much to handle and had to be moved to the tranquilised calm of the nursing home, Barnaby lost all interest in flowers.

'You know what a weed is?' he asked Jack.

Jack did but he guessed that Barnaby wasn't really interested in his opinion.

'A weed is a plant in the wrong place.'

'That's true,' said Jack who knew how to stay on Barnaby's good side.

'No point in all those flowers now that she's gone,' said Barnaby. 'No point in me paying you good money to look after something I don't much care for.'

'They're no trouble, and they are beautiful,' said Jack.

'You enjoy them don't you?'

Barnaby took a long hard look at his garden and then turned to stare at Jack, as if never really seeing him before. At last he said, 'You're one of those people who like things to look nice, aren't you?' Jack, as a gardener, was a bit perplexed by this as it was obviously meant as a criticism.

'Maybe,' he said.

'Keep the dahlia,' said Barnaby. 'They can go the church for flower arrangements. I like to see flowers in the church.' And sure enough, during the season, Barnaby kept the church supplied with the opulent blooms.

Trim the hedges and dig the drains.

Barnaby had made his money from owning a hotel but he had started life as a farmer and a farmer was what he instinctively was. He looked at his garden as a piece of land and he managed it, first and foremost, as a farmer would care for his holding. Hedges were to be kept in good order and drains in good repair. The fact that Barnaby's hedges and drains were what the public saw of his property was not lost on him. He didn't give a shit what people thought about him, but he cared immensely that they respected him.

Jack kept the hedges neat and tidy. Jack kept the drains that ran alongside those hedges clear and running free.

'You've missed a bit,' said Barnaby looking at a single bramble stalk that wavered up into the sky like an antenna searching for aliens.

'I can't reach it,' said Jack.

'I'll hold your ladder,' said Barnaby.

Jack looked at Barnaby's liver-spotted hands, his bird-thin shoulders and his trembling legs. 'It's fine,' he said.

'Get up there,' said Barnaby, holding the stepladder.

'I notice you're the one holding the ladder and I'm the one climbing,' said Jack who was less then comfortable with heights.

'I notice I'm the one who's paying you,' said Barnaby.

'Fuck,' said Jack, under his breath. Barnaby said nothing, acting a little more deaf than was usual.

The job with the drains was to cut out the weeds that clogged them and dig out the grit and silt that the rain washed into them and then barrow that down to the stream and tip it in. Most of that process was well and good but tipping barrow after barrow load of muck into the stream didn't sit all that well with Jack but, to be honest, his fear that Barnaby would find him not doing it was more motivating than the fact that one of the neighbours would find Jack doing it.

So the hedges and the drains got done, but they were very much a once-or-twice-a-year job.

Which brings us to chopping firewood.

Barnaby has had a number of cardiac events that have led him to feel the cold very easily. He has thin blood and it's pumped around his body by a tired heart. Sometimes Jack has touched his hand and it is like touching a corpse, it's that cold.

Barnaby can't risk getting cold, but he can't afford to stay warm either. Before he retired, Barnaby was a wealthy man. He owned a big hotel that looked out over the sea. For nine months a year it was packed full of pensioners and young families from the north of England coming for two weeks of fun and sun on the English Riviera. The hotel thrived, it was just the tourist industry that withered and died.

By the time Barnaby was 70 the hotel was almost

constantly empty and he decided to accept a property developer's offer. Barnaby divided the money – and it was a lot – between his two sons on the understanding that they would give him an income for life. The three of them decided what that sum should be and legal documents were drawn up and duly signed.

The thing is, inflation came along and ate almost all of Barnaby's income and the boys, presumably in revenge for being fathered by Barnaby, decided to stick to the letter of the agreement rather than its spirit. Barnaby wasn't starving but he wasn't well off and he was pushed back on to the knack he had always had for being careful with money.

Barnaby let it be known amongst the builders and tradesmen who worked locally that he would be more than happy if they dumped any scrap wood and timber from their projects in his drive. Getting rid of that sort of rubbish was the bane of most of their lives and so Barnaby's kind offer found a welcome audience. They knew that Barnaby was going to burn it in his wood-burner but they weren't overly fussy about what sort of rubbish they dumped, just as long as there was a wood element to it.

So, panels of chipboard with kitchen tiles still attached.

Window frames that were still glazed and had hinges and latches still in place.

Pallets. I mean really big, industrial pallets.

Furniture. Floor boards. A sofa. The pews from a church and a coat rack from a school.

'Some of this will burn pretty well,' said Jack.

'It all will,' said Barnaby.

'Well, maybe,' said Jack. 'I don't know that it will all cut up.'

'You can cut it up. We've got the saws. You can cut it

up in the garage.'

Barnaby had sold his car and bought a mobility scooter that now lived in a tiny shed next to the front door. That left the garage empty. Well, empty but for piles and piles of things that might come in useful. Barnaby was not a man to let things go to waste and sometimes it was difficult to decide what might be useful in the future and so he tended to ere on the side of caution and keep everything. The garage was panelled out with old 1950's angle iron shelving stacked high with stuff. From old tobacco tins to filling-cabinet draws, each container was carefully labelled as to its contents; "3/4inch bolts" and "galvanised nails", "washers" and "pump parts". There were two freestanding kitchen cupboards that had spewed out a load of hammers and planes, screwdrivers and chisels. A chest of drawers that contained plumbing fittings and empty boxes of weed killer. Down one wall was an avalanche of empty paint cans. Tucked up on the rafters were lengths of exhaust pipe, oilcans and a couple of rusty gas bottles. Back in the day, Barnaby had been the king of recycling. If you wanted swords beaten into ploughshares, or vice-versa, old Mr Abbott was your man.

There were also two saws. A reciprocating saw from the Kataba Tool Co. of Osaka that Jack considered an accident waiting to happen, and a pretty nasty accident at that, and the Makita chop saw. The Makita had been a precision carpenter's tool. It was now beaten and defeated and forced to chop up any old shit that was thrown at it. Jack sometimes saw it as a kindred spirit.

'Small enough to go on the fire, mind,' said Barnaby. 'And keep the kindling and the big stuff separate. You can put it in these old kitchen draws and I'll carry it through as I need it.'

Jack nodded.

'I can't afford the gas heating anymore. Those big bottles of Calor are over fifty pounds now and I can go through two a week. You need to do this for me.'

'Yeah, I know,' said Jack. 'Let's get it done, then,' and he pulled on his gloves and turned to the pile of rubbish that filled the drive.

When Jack came back to Barnaby's the following week he knocked on the kitchen door and waited for the old man to appear. After a couple of minutes he heard slippers shuffling across the tiled floor and the blurred outline of Barnaby slowly came into focus as he came closer to the frosted glass.

'What are we doing this week?' he asked when the door finally opened.

'Cutting wood,' said Barnaby.

'You can't have finished all that. I did loads. And it hasn't even been all that cold.'

'Feel,' said Barnaby and held out his hand.

Jack frowned at the corpse-cold handshake and looked more closely at the old man, the grey stubble that hung on in patches around his face, the red rims to his eyes that made the pallor all the more apparent, the large blob of congealed egg on his jacket next to the badge proclaiming, "Jesus is Lord".

'Are you alright?' he asked.

'I just need to get warm. If I can keep warm I'll be alright.'

The heap of builders' rubbish that Barnaby euphemistically called "the wood pile" had grown considerably and Jack set to starting with the bits that seemed likely to give him least trouble.

The Makita growled and chewed at lengths of rafters ripped from a derelict cottage. It struggled with the awkward puzzle of taking a rocking chair to pieces. It gnawed its way through nail-studded skirting board like an electric mouse.

'Here,' said Barnaby handing Jack a huge gnarled tree root.

'It won't touch that.'

'Find a way,' said Barnaby. 'I need to burn all of this. I need to be warm.'

'I thought your faith would keep you warm,' said Jack and regretted it instantly.

'I believe in God and yes, I pray. I pray that the Lord will provide. And what he's provided me with so far is that pile of wood and you, so you just get on and do the Lord's work if that's the way you want to see it.'

And Jack got back to chopping wood.

That next week the weather got colder and when Jack knocked on the kitchen door he found he had another job to do before he got to play with the Makita again.

Barnaby handed him a big role of clear, polyethylene sheet, some battening, a hammer and a mixed bag of nails and screws. 'I need to make the house warmer. Put this over all the windows in the front room. Just batten it to the window frames. It'll work like double-glazing. Put it over my bedroom window as well.'

Jack pursed his lips and bobbed his head about. 'It could work,' he said. 'I'll get my cordless for the screws.'

'There's a hammer,' said Barnaby. 'Drive them in with the hammer, it'll be quicker and then you can get more wood cut.'

'Dear God,' muttered Jack under his breath but Barnaby heard him and gave him a withering look.

'Sorry,' said Jack, 'and I'm sorry about last week.' Barnaby frowned at him. 'What I said when I was here last week, about your faith. I'm sorry, I shouldn't have said that.'

'Well,' said Barnaby,' you don't believe, do you? But I do,' and he closed the kitchen door in Jack's face.

While he was hammering screws into window frames and cutting sheets of plastic into makeshift double-glazing units Jack considered Barnaby's faith. This house, the home his wife was in and the church in the village were really the only places where Barnaby lived his life. They divided him into equal thirds and together they made up all he was. Barnaby's faith was hard and unyielding. Barnaby's faith was a bone running through his body. The Lord was no more a mystery to Barnaby than had been a cow in a field or a guest in a hotel lobby.

When he'd finished his work, Jack knocked once again on the kitchen door. There was a symbol of the fish next to the Neighbourhood Watch sticker; pragmatic Barnaby warding off all evil.

'I'm off now,' said Jack when the door opened and he held out his hand for his money.

'I hope you've cut enough,' said Barnaby. 'It's due to be bitter this weekend. Cold as charity,' and he allowed himself a thin smile.

And so it proved to be.

There was no snow or frost but rather a deep, damp cold that sucked the warmth out of the earth. It threatened to suck the life out of Barnaby. When he opened the door to Jack, the old man was not only wearing his jacket, collar and tie as he always did, but also a thick blanket dressing gown and a knitted bobble-hat on his pate. His eyes were unfocussed and his mouth hung open a little.

'Oh, no,' murmured Jack and stepped into the kitchen, taking Barnaby by the arm he led him to a kitchen chair and got him to sit down. The house seemed warm enough but Barnaby felt like a block of ice.

'Do you want a cup of tea?' asked Jack, flicking the kettle on. 'You should see the Doctor. I'll run you down in the van.'

'I'm fine. I'm fine,' said Barnaby and then he coughed up a great, green lump of phlegm that ran down his chin and dripped onto his tie.

'Hey, it's OK,' said Jack. 'It's going to be OK.' But Barnaby started coughing again and his body was wracked with the struggle. From the kitchen wall an old print of Jesus surrounded by a fading golden halo looked quietly and benignly down.

'I need to…' He coughed again. 'I just need to… Oh, my God,' and Barnaby pulled himself up and started to limp towards the door that led to the downstairs toilet. Jack didn't know what to do; he held Barnaby's arm in one strong hand and pushed the toilet door open for him. Barnaby lurched toward the toilet and lent over it. The coughing became steady and regular, like a timeworn tractor trying to start on a flat battery. Barnaby put his head down the toilet and retched. Jack turned away.

'It's OK. Hey, it's OK,' but Jack didn't know which one of them he was actually saying that to.

Barnaby straightened up. His face seemed thin and shrunken and he had tears in his eyes. Staring at Jack, he slowly shook his head in horror but it wasn't until he began to try and speak that Jack realised what had happened.

'Go into the kitchen, he said to Barnaby. 'Go and sit down. I'll get them,' and he rolled up the sleeve on his right hand and looked down at Barnaby's dentures sitting in the bottom of the toilet bowl.

Twenty minutes later, Barnaby was sitting in his chair by the fire in the front room and Jack was feeding the last few logs onto the blaze.

'You're a good man,' said Barnaby quietly.

'Bullshit,' said Jack. 'Anyone would have…'

'No. They wouldn't.' Barnaby rubbed at the dirt and ash on the threadbare carpet with his slippered foot. His head rocked from side to side. 'Faith gives you strength, but if it's just strength to endure, what is the point? I never see my boys, Margaret is never coming out of that home and I will never feel warm again,' and a sad little laugh slipped past his thin, purple lips. Barnaby's eyes flicked up to a cheap painting of the Ascension above the fireplace. There were dusty, palm crosses tucked into the frame. 'He's all right for a bit of compassion but Old Nick is the one with the fires and that's what I need now. I need a roaring fire.'

'Don't be daft,' said Jack.

'No, you said it. You said my faith should keep me warm. Well, it doesn't. At least, not warm enough.' Barnaby looked at his watch. 'You've still got half an hour,' he said. 'Cut me some more wood, please.'

'I'll fill the drawers up for you. I think I can stretch to that,' and Jack took the old man's hand and squeezed it. 'You'll be OK,' he said without much hope.

The cold spell persevered over the following week and Jack dreaded what he might find when it was time for him to knock by the symbol of the fish again.

'You look better,' he said when the door opened and to some extent he meant it. There was a little more colour in Barnaby's cheeks and, although he still had his knitted hat on, he wasn't wearing the dressing gown.

'Don't come in, I've just swept the floor,' said Barnaby when Jack moved towards the kitchen step and the old man even put a hand out to stop him.

Jack shrugged. 'Chop some wood then, is it?'

'The greenhouse,' said Barnaby. 'Take the dead tomatoes out of the greenhouse.' And then he seemed to catch himself. 'Then chop the wood. Yes, yes then chop me some more wood, please,' and Barnaby swung the door closed in Jack's face. 'Got to keep the heat in,' Jack heard him say and, do you know, the kitchen had felt warmer than usual for that minute Jack had stood at the open door.

Half an hour later the tomato plants were on the compost heap and Jack was in the garage chopping wood when Barnaby came shuffling through the door that led to the house.

'That plastic sheet worked, then,' said Jack.

Barnaby frowned at him.

'The double-glazing stuff that we put up last week, it must have worked. You've not used as much wood.'

Barnaby nodded but Jack saw that his attention was elsewhere. He turned to look where the old man was looking and on the workbench was a pump and a tangle of pipe. One of the empty, rusty gas bottles had a length of steel pipe attached where the valve had been but what caught Jack's eye was the other end of that. The two-inch piping had melted like a church candle and a trickle of molten steel ran down its length.

Chewing his lip, Jack turned back to Barnaby but the old man was holding out a couple of ten-pound notes in one bruised and liver-spotted hand.

'Off you go then,' he said. Jack shrugged, said thank you and left.

Seven days later, Jack was back.

It had been another cold week, the temperature dropping down to just a few degrees during the day and colder at night.

The little shed by the front door was open and Barnaby's mobility scooter was missing so Jack let himself into the garage thinking that all the chopped firewood would be gone and he better get to work with the Makita. When the garage door rolled up, Jack just stood there for a moment and rubbed at the stubble on his chin. He didn't believe in miracles, so this just counted as a puzzle.

The garage was warm but hardly any of the firewood had gone.

Jack pushed against the door that led through into the house, but it was locked. Even through the closed door he could feel the heat on the other side. The house was toasty. Jack looked around, scratching at his head and trying to piece the jigsaw together.

The pump, gas bottle and piping that had been on the workbench was gone but leaning next to it were some lengths of industrial heating pipe that Barnaby had obviously salvaged from some builder's contribution to the "wood pile". A big wheel-turned valve and a pile of asbestos insulation lay on the garage floor.

'Well, fuck me,' murmured Jack to himself.

When Barnaby returned home he found Jack cutting firewood and piling it in the corner of the garage. All the usual kitchen draws were full.

'I was at church. It's Ash Wednesday,' said Barnaby.

Jack raised an eyebrow and nodded towards the woodpile. 'How appropriate.'

'I thought I'd be back before you got here.'

'How come you've not used all the wood? The house seems pretty warm.'

Barnaby frowned. 'My boys bought me a couple of bottles of Calor gas. They were worried so they bought me some gas and I've been using that and it's kept me warm enough so that's all right. You don't need to worry. I'm all right. Why don't you leave this and tidy the greenhouse. Yes, that's a good idea now that the tomatoes are gone. That would be good. I've got your money,' and Barnaby held out a pair of ten-pound notes. When Jack took them he noticed a vicious burn on Barnaby's wrist but didn't say anything.

When Jack had finished with the greenhouse he went looking for Barnaby, knocking at the kitchen door and peering in through the windows but the old man was nowhere to be seen. There was steam pouring out of the flue that led from the boiler though.

Jack was just about to get in his van and depart for another week when he gave in to the thoughts that had been crawling around his head for the last hour. The big 47kg propane bottles lived just inside the garden fence, chained to a concrete post and hooked up to the feed pipe that led to the boiler.

Jack gave each one a little push. They were all empty. They were old and dirty and empty. The boys hadn't bought him any gas; they'd probably not even been here. And yet the boiler was running.

Another week.

Seven more days.

Jack did a lot of thinking in that time. Barnaby was heating his house. That heat was coming from somewhere, but where? And what the hell had he been making in the garage?

The old man had a habit of doing things his way and Barnaby's way wasn't always the safest or most sensible. Barnaby was a man who thought it made sense to hammer screws in if that saved time. Barnaby wasn't someone you would want as a domestic heating engineer.

In the van, on the way to Barnaby's house, Jack made his mind up.

'I thought the drains needed doing, they looked like they needed doing,' said Barnaby as soon as he opened the door.

'Yeah, I bet you did,' said Jack and pushed his way inside then, 'Jesus Christ, what is going on?'

The ancient Baxi boiler that hung on the kitchen wall had its cover levered off and its mutilated guts left on show. Crumbly slabs of yellowed glass-wool insulation had been ripped apart and the blackened boiler tank was wrapped with thick, copper piping. Blue and red electric wiring had been torn loose and the gas burner itself was lying on the floor of the cabinet. Pipes ran down from the ruined boiler and disappeared through a hole that had been roughly hacked in the floorboards. There were burn marks scorching the wallpaper up from the hole. The picture of Christ and his golden glow was turned to the wall.

'What have you done?' asked Jack.

'Nothing. I've done nothing…'

'It doesn't look like nothing.'

'I lied about the gas.'

'I know. That's fucking obvious. What on earth have you been doing?'

There was the acrid stench of sulfur coming from somewhere and a noise, a deep droning sonorous bass that came and went in slow waves. And something else, Jack could hear something else but his brain seemed to be trying desperately to ignore it.

'I used that old pump,' said Barnaby. 'You know, the one that Caroline from across the road gave me. I tried the old pond-pump first but...'

'The heat, where's the heat coming from? What's down there?' and Jack pointed at the hole in the floorboards.

Barnaby put his hands on the kitchen table to steady himself and he leant towards Jack. 'Please just leave it,' he said. 'You've been a good friend. Just leave it.'

Jack shook his head, partly to say "no" and partly out of frustration and puzzlement but also to clear it from that abnormal sound that was trying to climb through his ears and into his mind and the smell; that bitter, foul stench. 'I need to see,' he said.

'No you don't,' said Barnaby. 'Just leave it, I beg you. In the name of God... Just leave it,' and Jack cringed as the bass note became a landslide of sound that buried Barnaby's last few words. Was that a tear in the old man's eye or was it a bead of sweat? Christ but it was hot in the kitchen.

Jack pushed past Barnaby's bone-thin frame towards the door to the rest of the house. On the other side was a hall with a staircase leading upwards and an open door showing a flight of rougher wooden stairs leading down. Jack turned through the door and began to descend. The heat made Jack's skin crawl. The heat and the noise hit him in waves and over the waves like screaming gulls were the higher notes of sound that he still couldn't put a name to. At the foot of the cellar steps Jack eventually gave in to the reek of sulfur and vomited on the rammed earth floor. Barnaby stepped past him and handed him a clean, linen handkerchief.

'At first I'd just come and sit down here when I got too cold. No matter how much wood I put on the fire, it was as if the heat never really reached me, but this? I could feel the heat from this.'

At first Jack thought that he was looking at a log burner in the darkened cellar because all he could see was a floating wall of flame; a rolling, roaring window of fire that appeared to sit against the cellar's end wall but either his eyes became more accustomed to the light or his brain finally admitted the truth of the horror that he was looking at.

At the end of the cellar there was a rent in the fabric of reality and on the other side of it was the damnation and endless torment that was Hell.

Jack made a sickly gurgling sound in the back of his throat as the fibers and structures that held his consciousness together began to melt.

'God is real, so I knew the Devil was real too,' he heard Barnaby say. 'There's a heaven so there must be a hell. And there is.'

Jack sagged to the floor. He knew what the other noise was now and the knowledge gutted him. Screams. He was hearing the endless screams of millions of tormented souls as they burned away to gas heating Barnaby's home.

'Look what I had to do,' said Barnaby nudging the other man. 'It wasn't easy. You could help me make it better.' Barnaby pointed at the piping that crawled across the cellar floor. Flange joints in the industrial heating pipes that dipped through the rent were held together with wire and bent nails. The pump balanced on a bald tyre and the pipe leading up to the kitchen was lagged with handfuls of asbestos held in place with lengths of carpet.

Jack turned to look at Barnaby, his eyes wide with horror. 'What have you fuckin' done, man?' he howled. 'It's got to go.'

'If you help me, if we work together, we can…'

'No, not the bloody plumbing,' whispered Jack. 'That,' and he pointed at the gate to Hell.

For a moment or two, Barnaby was completely still and silent and then he shook himself and sighed. 'I can't be cold again. I just can't. I think that when I go, this will close again. Till then, I need it.'

Jack was squatting just in front of the rent, his face reddened from the heat, eyes wide and mouth slack. 'Can't,' was the only word that escaped him.

'Better stoke the fire then,' said Barnaby and gave Jack a little push before turning to walk back upstairs. He thought, at first, that perhaps he could pick Jack's scream out from the others but as he climbed the cellar steps he wasn't so sure.

BRAMBLE

'YOU DON'T talk about her much.'

'I think about her though. We were so close when she was little.'

'She's little now,' said ToePick.

'No,' said Bramble. 'She's a woman now.'

'A little one. She's only, what? How old? Fifteen, sixteen?'

'Something like,' said Bramble.

'She still livin' around here?'

'Yeah, I think so. But I haven't seen her for months.'

'Shame,' said ToePick and Bramble nodded his head.

They walked on in silence but for the sound of their boots crunching through the autumn leaves on the path.

'Not much further, is it?' asked ToePick after a while.

'No,' said Bramble. 'Across the common and then we're pretty much there. Why?'

'It's gonna rain.'

'Oh, for fuck…Really?'

'Yeah. I can hear it. Listen.'

Bramble cocked his head and sure enough, rain, like bored fingers tapping on a taut drum skin and getting quickly closer.

Bramble flipped his hood over his head and pulled it snug around his face. 'Come on then,' he said. 'Let's step out.'

The two of them lengthened their stride and ToePick sank his neck into his massive shoulders. Within a few minutes they were struggling through a bitter-cold squall that neither Bramble's hoodie nor ToePick's shoulders did much to protect them from. They were both well and truly soaked by the time they reached the edge of the common and could see the lights of the estate amongst the trees.

'I should be tucked up in my bed. Or at least trying to get into someone else's,' grumbled Bramble.

'You know how it is,' said ToePick. 'The Waverley calls and we come running.'

'Yeah well, could have called on a slightly nicer night.'

'It's easing up, isn't it?'

'Let's wait here a minute, then,' said Bramble and he dropped his backpack at the base of a tree and sat down next to it. ToePick sat down beside him. Bramble tugged the edge of his hood to one side so that he could look up at the big man. ToePick's beard was dripping water and his top-knot looked like a pile of seaweed clinging to the rock of his shaved head.

'What?' said ToePick.

'Oh, nothin',' said Bramble. 'Ever thought of getting a hat?'

'They don't suit me.'

'I'm not sure your fuckin' clothes suit you but it doesn't mean you have to run around bare-ass naked in the freezing rain, does it?'

ToePick grunted. 'I wonder what The Waverley wants,'

he said.

'Someone scared, someone hurt, someone reminded of how things are.'

'Hmm. Ain't right, is it?'

'Better we do it than someone else, eh? Some of the young ones out to make their bones. Nasty fuckers, they really are.'

'S'pose,' said ToePick, and started cleaning his fingernails with the tip of a small shank. ToePick flicked dirt off the end of his blade and then spat on the ground between his feet. 'Come on,' he said. 'Let's go.'

Bramble picked himself up off the ground and watched ToePick moving through the wood. It was like watching a bear go for a stroll. ToePick was huge. Not a giant, possibly, but a very big man. A man who never worried over questions like, 'Is this heavy?' or 'Will these people hurt me?' ToePick never had to ask himself things like that. It just never occurred in his world and perhaps because of that he was almost always amiable. Well, it would probably be more accurate to say, 'often amiable'.

Bramble smiled at the broad back of his friend and then set off to follow him.

They followed the path across the common. The grass had been trampled flat by passing feet, the ground churned up into a track of mud, sludge and puddles. Hailstones lay in little drifts across the bare earth and rabbit droppings peppered the grass. As they reached the estate side of the common the sun slumped beneath the horizon and within a few minutes almost all that could be seen of The Wood was the angry black pen-scratches of bare trees scribbled furiously over and over against the purple-grey sky. The first trees grew gnarled and weather lashed but as they went deeper into The Wood they became taller and straighter, more like the solid pillars that the estate was built around.

'Over there, to the right, isn't it?' muttered ToePick pointing at a flickering light. Bramble was about to reply when three figures stepped out of the murk. 'What you doin' here, eh?' said a voice. 'You're not from around here. Don't know your fuckin' face.'

ToePick looked slightly puzzled as if, not for the first time, he was mulling over just how stupid some of his fellow human beings could be. His chin came up, head slightly on one side, and he peered at the three but Bramble seemed to relax. Bramble's eyes twinkled and a crooked smile slowly spread across his face. His fingers stretched and he rolled his shoulders.

The three men in front of them were all hoods and fur collars, thick belts and boots with too many buckles. Even standing still, they swaggered, swaying around to some deep-buried beat. One of them took a long pull on a thick jabba blunt before passing it on.

'So wotcha' doin' on the 'state, man?'

'We're here to see the Wa...' began ToePick but Bramble hushed him.

'We are little lambs who have lost our way,' said Bramble softly.

'You what? You fuckin' jokin' me, man,' said the biggest of the three. 'I'll fuckin' slice you. I swear to fuck, I will.'

'Ooh, you wouldn't hurt an old man, would you,' said Bramble stepping in front of ToePick and up closer to the three. 'No really, I mean it. Would you hurt an old man?'

'I'll fuckin' cut you. Cut you deep, old man,' growled the buck and he let a long blade slide from his sleeve and shine like cruelty in the darkness.

Bramble dropped his hips an inch or two, sitting down into a fighting stance. Smiling, he nodded his head to one side. A question. A challenge. The beginning to a dance. A dance Bramble enjoyed so very much.

'Bramble, don't,' said ToePick, 'they're just kids.'

'What? What you call him? What you fucking call him?'

'I was only going to tease them,' said Bramble.

'Yeah, right,' said ToePick.

'Fuck, man,' said the buck. 'I didn't know. On my fuckin' mother, I didn't know.'

'We've come to see the Waverley,' said ToePick and not one of the three seemed to have any problem with that at all.

.

ToePick stretched and yawned and tried to fart discreetly under the furs and blankets. He bundled up his shirt and stuffed it between his head and the wooden wall behind him as a pillow and pulled a corner up over his chest covering the heavy slabs of muscle and the curls and twists of greying hair.

'Two eggs do you, or do you want three?' asked Bramble.

ToePick just grunted.

Bramble was standing by the log burner chopping mushrooms on a round of oak as the skillet warmed on top of the stove, a golden pebble of butter melting away on the black iron of the pan. The blade flew through the dark gilled ceps and Bramble left it point-first quivering in the block as he turned to look at ToePick.

'I wouldn't have done anything,' said Bramble. 'I don't do that anymore.'

ToePick looked at him from behind a puzzled frown.

'The kids,' said Bramble. 'The three kids.'

'Oh, them.'

'Yeah. Even this guy we're going to see…'

'This guy the Waverley wants us to teach a lesson. That one, yeah?'

'Yeah. That one. I don't want to hurt him.'

'I'm sure that will be a great comfort to him as you get to work,' said ToePick swinging a leg out of the bed.

Bramble started cracking shells on the side of a bowl, breaking eggs to make an omelette. 'It's Berry,' he said. 'I don't like the thought of her knowing that this is what her old man does. I don't like it.'

'You hardly ever see her.'

'I don't like that, either.'

ToePick stood up and scratched at his groin through his leggings then took a few steps across the room.

'You're not, are you?' said Bramble as he slid the mushrooms into the hot pan.

'What?'

'Are you going to piss off the balcony?'

'Err, no,' said ToePick and changed direction towards where the piss-pot was.

Half an hour later the two of them were on the balcony nursing mugs of tea and looking out over the estate. The flop that they were in was on the top floor of the high-house so they were right up amongst the canopy; a hundred, perhaps a hundred and twenty feet above the ground. The trunks of the trees above them were too thin to support another floor and so they could look up through the last few leafless branches and see the grey sky and the few darker smears of cloud that rolled across it.

Each high-house looked like a jumble of wooden boxes that had been stuck amongst the towering trees. Roofs kicked off at odd angles, balconies and stairways, shuttered windows and rope sways seemed random and higgle-piggle because that was what they were. No high-house had ever been planned, they just grew in the trees like colossal fungus. Tree houses that happened to be ten or more stories high. Timber tower blocks.

'Go and find him then, shall we?' said ToePick.

'Yeah, I guess so. The Waverley said he'd crashed in the drink-hole.'

'Let's start there then,' said ToePick and let the dregs of his tea spill over the balcony.

.

The drink-hole was only three stories high but at some point an owner had built on a couple of fat-bellied, bow fronted windows to make it look a bit smarter, made a broad wooden staircase up to the first floor so that customers could get in easily and hung out a shingle with a picture of two mugs of beer on it in case anyone was in any doubt about what the drink-hole had for sale.

Bramble and ToePick climbed the staircase carefully, stepping over a puddle of vomit and what appeared to be a pile of cat shit.

The main bar was dark and sordid-looking with a wooden floor and panelled walls. There were tables, chairs and stools around the walls and clustered in front of the big, empty fireplace. At the back of the room was the bar itself and above that was a gallery that could be reached by a twisting staircase of treads cut into a stout tree trunk.

The place looked empty. Candles had burnt out. Lamp-wicks been snuffed out. Two shafts of sunlight speared down to the floor from a pair of high windows and an entire galaxy of dust swam in their beams. The bar stank of sweat, beer and the sweet smell of jabba.

Bramble looked at ToePick and grimaced. 'Nice.'

Like a ghoul rising from the grave a thin, pale figure slowly stood up from behind the bar. He was about to open his mouth when Bramble tapped his lips with his finger and ToePick slowly shook his great head. The two of them walked unhurriedly across the room until they reached the bar. ToePick perched on a stool while Bramble steepled his fingers as if about to pray then leant towards the gaunt figure and rested his elbows on the zinc bar top, their two faces nose to nose. 'Greycat,' he said quietly. 'Youngish, dark hair, big mouth and holding a pile of jabba that, it turns out, isn't his.' Bramble raised his eyebrows in question. 'Ring any bells at all?'

The barman began to shrug when ToePick let a shank appear in his hand and dragged the tip down the length of the bar top making a noise like cat's claws on slate. The emaciated barman looked at the knifepoint cutting easily through the grey metal, gulped and then pointed upwards to the gallery. 'Door on the left,' he murmured and wet his dry lips with the tip of his grey, furred tongue. Bramble punched him hard in the temple and he collapsed behind the bar like a pile of empty clothes. "What?' said Bramble when he saw ToePick looking at him. 'Don't want to be disturbed, do we?'

The two of them climbed the twisting stair up to the gallery. They barely made a sound until they were standing in front of the left-hand door. ToePick nodded at the wooden door and raised a questioning eyebrow.

'Oh, go on then,' said Bramble and with a tiny squeak of joy ToePick kicked the door as hard as he could. The door shattered into half a dozen planks and a broken latch. ToePick and Bramble only had to step over the pile of what was now firewood and they were in the room.

A naked man sprang up from beneath a pile of rags and blankets. His mouth and eyes gaping wide open in blank surprise. 'No,' said ToePick and pushed him hard back down into the fart-sack. The man's mouth opened even wider and he took in a great chest full of air. ToePick closed his other hand over his face and squeezed. The man's eyes bulged but not a sound escaped him.

Bramble sat down on the edge of the bed's platform and smiled. "Greycat, I take it,' he said.

Holding tight with the huge vice of his hand, ToePick wobbled the man's head up and down so that he nodded vigorously. Bramble grunted, 'Let him answer for himself, eh.' ToePick chuckled and let go of Greycat's head.

'I'm led to believe,' said Bramble. 'That someone has stolen a great deal of jabba from a dealer who stupidly enjoyed too much of his own product.' Greycat opened his mouth again but Bramble raised a finger. 'Let me finish,' he said. 'I don't know if this was a crime of opportunity or the result of remorseless planning by a master criminal. But I do know that the person who did it was you. I assume that you have stashed the haul somewhere safe and you plan to sell it later.'

Greycat raised his eyebrows and leant forward a little.

'Shut. The fuck. Up,' said Bramble. ToePick flicked Greycat's ear with a massive finger. Greycat whimpered.

'The jabba belongs to the Waverley,' said Bramble

and Greycat's face collapsed into misery. 'I work for the Waverley. You can see where this is going, can't you?'

'Please, can I...' said Greycat. ToePick flicked his ear, much harder this time.

'No, you can't' said Bramble. 'So what I should do now, see, is start torturing you. Have you ever been tortured?' Greycat shook his head emphatically.

'Right. Right, of course not. Well, it starts with me stabbing you a few times with this.' A long, thin shank appeared in Bramble's hand. 'And quite a while later I hold your face against that hot stove over there'. Bramble nodded towards a small log-burner in a corner of the room. 'I'm hazy about the details in between but I think it involves you screaming quite a lot.'

Greycat looked aghast, like a corpse desperate to get back into its grave.

'But I'm trying to be a nicer person,' continued Bramble. ToePick snorted in laughter and had to wipe the snot from his nose. Bramble frowned.

'Trying to be a better person,' said Bramble slowly and clearly. 'So I'm going to give you a chance to answer first. Where did you hide the jabba?'

'Over there, in that sack,' said Greycat and nodded at a big gunny-cloth bag leaning against the wall.

'Oh for fuck's sake,' said Bramble and ToePick laughed and laughed and laughed.

.

'She's definitely in the Oaks then,' said Bramble. 'You've seen her?'

'I haven't,' said Freja. 'But my girl saw her there

yesterday. She was shacked up with some young blade. Don't see no reason why she wouldn't still be there.'

Bramble nodded his head then scratched at his chin. ToePick hefted the gunny-cloth bag higher up on his shoulder and Freja rolled her eyes and groaned in exasperation as her youngest tugged at her hand and moaned, 'Mom, come on, let's go.' The four of them stood at the foot of the drink-hole staircase. They had met Freja as they'd been leaving.

'I need to go and see Berry,' said Bramble to ToePick. 'Go and see the Waverley, say it's all sorted, and give her this shit back,' and Bramble swung the gunnysack over to his friend. ToePick nodded and he went one way and Bramble another.

The Oaks was one of the bigger high-houses. It had been part of the estate for a good long time and had reached that stage where it was falling apart and being rebuilt simultaneously. The only way up from the ground was by a spiral staircase that wound around one of the monumental tree trunks. Bramble stood for a moment at its base and looked up. He picked at his teeth then started biting one of his nails before he realised he was just trying to put off the moment. With a grunt he stepped on to the first tread of the staircase and began to climb.

The stair twisted upwards giving Bramble a view out over the estate and a chance to look inwards at the levels of the Oaks and the people living there. Washing was hung out to dry and bedding out to air; draped over balcony rails and the strong ropes that supported the sways. People shouted gossip from one level to another and shared each other's secrets at the top of their voices. Lover's names and gang sign were scratched into the timber of the trees. Women squatted in the middle of the walkways chopping vegetables and grinding seed. From a room on the third level came the loud guttural moaning and breathy whimpers of a woman being solidly fucked. A baby cried somewhere further up and a gang of boys started making a ruckus on the ground beneath the high-house, kicking a bladder against the trunks.

The Oaks was like a warren dug out of the earth and perched up in the canopy, a vast den where everyone who lived there just about got on. Just about. Bramble looked this way and that, peered into open doors and snatched a glance through un-shuttered windows. Not knowing where Berry might be found, not even if she was here at all. By the time he reached the fifth level he had just about given up hope of finding her when something familiar caught his eye. There was a patchwork blanket spread out on the balcony rail. It was Berry's.

Nervously, Bramble looked about. 'Berry?' he said quietly.

He turned and saw her through an open door. She stood on some stairs leading up to a sleeping platform. She was only wearing a short cotton shift. She looked at Bramble, as haughty as a princess and as angry as a cat.

'What?' she said.

Is that it, thought Bramble? After all these months, just one word?

'Hi,' he said. 'How are you?' But he was looking at her. Could see more of her than he really wanted to. He could see the bruises at the tops of her thighs and the bags under her eyes and the fact that her skin looked sallow and unwashed.

'Don't look at me like that,' she said, cold with contempt

for opportunities missed and responsibilities avoided.

'Can I come in?' asked Bramble. Berry said nothing. She walked down the last couple of stairs and sat down on a pile of fat cushions in the far corner of the room. She pulled a blanket over her bare knees but Bramble had already seen the scratches down the back of one leg and a bruise at the top of her arm where a man's fingers would go if he were holding her. He plucked up his courage and stepped inside.

'Stop it,' she spat. 'Stop looking at me.'

Bramble looked down at the boards, out of the window, he looked at the stair. Was the owner of the fingers up there? The man who had given his daughter those purple and blue blooms?

'Did Mamay send you? I hate her.'

'I just came…'

'Why? Go now.'

'I need to know that you are alright.'

'Why?'

Bramble winced.

'Why? She asked. 'So you can get on with your life without feeling guilty about me? Well, you can. There is someone who looks after me. There's someone who loves me.'

'Looks like it,' said Bramble and then actually rocked back as she glared at him.

'Fuck you,' she hurled the words at him so hard they would have split stone.

'Sorry, I…'

'Sorry,' she hissed. 'There isn't enough sorry in the world. Fuck you and your sorry'.

Bramble felt a tear in his eye. He spread his arms, palms

up, as an entreaty, begging for a hug, not for her but for him. 'I love you,' he whispered.

'I have someone who loves me,' she said. 'You know how I know that he loves me? Because he's there with me, he's in my life. He holds me. He isn't you.'

Bramble searched for the words to say. He thought of the first word and then the next word and the one after that but then every sentence that he tried out in his head turned to ash. Every excuse and every reason crashed like storm-tossed ships on the rocks of her cold fury.

'I…' he said.

'No,' she spat, 'not you. Me. Try starting with me.'

Bramble sagged to the floor, he sat at her feet and thought nothing more of that other than it seemed right. 'You,' he said. He squeezed his eyes tight shut. Somewhere inside himself was a truth that would solve this, somewhere inside himself was an answer that would take away the hurt. And even as he thought that, he knew that it was his own, selfish hurt that he mostly wanted gone.

'You and I were so close. Best friends. I carried you everywhere. We were never not together. For all your life. Apart from this last little bit.'

Berry made a tiny cry and when Bramble looked at her he could see the awful, awful pain in her eyes. 'But this last bit is all I remember,' she said. 'These last years are so much more of my life than they are of yours. It's like you've not been here for me for ever.'

'We can try,' said Bramble.

'No.' And then she said, 'Perhaps.'

'This man…' he began.

'Stop it,' said Berry. 'He's going to get some money. He's going to look after me, look after us. I want you to go now, please. Please just go.'

Bramble slowly stood up. He patted his pockets. He wanted to give her something. He found a shank and some knuckle-dusters. He felt numbed, as if he'd been beaten. He pulled a fat gold ring off his index finger; it had a big yellow Citrine set in it. He held the ring out to Berry but could think of nothing to say that would make any sense to either of them. She took the ring and turned away without giving him the hug he so badly wanted.

.

Bramble woke with a sore head. He might be trying to be a better person, but it seemed that he was taking it one step at a time.

'Oh, you're actually alive,' said ToePick. 'Fuck me.'

'Did I..?' asked Bramble.

'Yes, you did' said ToePick. 'You did all of it and more. You did all the jabba you got from Slim Pete and the whisky that Agneta was saving and then you and Agneta…'

'All right. I get it.'

'And from what we could all hear, so did Agneta.'

'Oh, god,' moaned Bramble and pulled the fur up over his head.

An hour later, Bramble and ToePick were getting their things together and preparing to leave. ToePick poured the last of his tea onto the hot ashes in the wood burner. Bramble nudged the piss-pot with his boot; someone else could take care of that.

'I'm sorry it didn't go so good with Berry,' said ToePick.

'I dunno', said Bramble. 'We talked. Perhaps we can talk again and then…'

'But you reckon she was doing jabba and fucking this guy.'

'Yeah.'

'Did she say?'

'No,' said Bramble. 'But it looked like.'

'You sure that it isn't,' said ToePick hesitantly, 'that all you wanted to do at that age was smoke jabba and have sex. It's what you would do if you were her. Pretty much all you do now, really.'

'Not funny,' said Bramble and the two of them picked up their stuff and began to make their way down to the ground.

At the foot of the stairs there was a woman waiting for them. She had thick grey hair piled up in a cloud on her head. Her arms were folded over a generous chest and her deep red brocade dress clung to her hips. Her face was strong boned and her sensual mouth sneered at Bramble.

'When I said, make sure he doesn't steal from me again,' said the Waverley, 'I didn't want a fucking promise. I didn't want him to pinky-swear and I didn't want him to cross his heart and hope to fuckin' die.'

'You got your shit back. He won't do it again,' said Bramble. 'I guarantee it.'

'That's true,' laughed the Waverley, 'because we went back and saw him last night while you were having your little party. And you are right, he won't do it again.'

She clicked her fingers and one of the men standing behind her stepped forward. It was the leader of the three that Bramble and ToePick had met two nights ago. He handed the Waverley a canvas sack and the Waverley threw it to Bramble. It squished, when he caught it.

Bramble's stomach turned over. He knew what was in

the bag just by the feel but he knew she was going to make him look.

The Waverley nodded her head and Bramble opened the bag. The man's hands had been severed at the wrist. There was a film of blood across their dirty-white flesh and over the gleaming ivory bones but then Bramble saw what else was there.

On one of the fingers was a chunky gold ring and set into it, gleaming beneath the blood, was a bright yellow Citrine stone.

THE SPIRE

Imagine a dream at the edge of a desert.
A meeting place for the timeless and the future.
Palm International Real Estate. © 2024

DAVID WOKE, and he woke as he did every morning. He woke in fear.

He kept his eyes closed. He took his first, slow fully conscious breath. He could smell no smoke and hear no screaming and yet he awoke feeling the fear of those things.

David lay in his silk pyjamas. He felt their smoothness against his skin.

He moved his fingertips a fraction of an inch and he felt the soft Egyptian cotton of his bed linen.

He took another, deeper breath and was aware of the cool, odourless air that the fans pushed into the room. He became mindful of the fact that he could hear those fans and the reason that he could hear them was that there was no other sound at all.

David was aware of all these things and he woke to another fear, the fear that they may end. That one morning all this might no longer be true.

Another breath and he opened his eyes. And all he saw was blackness.

David's eyes searched for something to focus on but there were no lights on in his room and no light outside it. He waited. Lying perfectly still, his head propped on a pillow he waited. He could now see a line in the blackness; the blind-dark was divided in two by something that hadn't been there a moment or a minute or an hour before.

There was now light.

A purple hue that brightened to midnight blue, a dark blue, an Egyptian blue while the earth remained as black as sin. The heavens and the earth became two separate and distinct things and then heaven began to glow. It glowed with a pure white that warmed to rose madder on the day's first tendrils of cloud. It brightened. The glow sucked the clouds into it, began to pull the blackness from the sky and burn it. In the sky's furnace, the blackness was consumed, burned brighter and brighter until the sky was ablaze.

David squinted as the sun broke the horizon at last, an oxyacetylene flame splitting heaven and earth apart, a cutting-torch opening the new day. Light flooded down from heaven and showed the earth for what it was. The rolling, dry ocean of the Namib desert, a sea of dunes and breaking waves of sand

David sat in his bed, fit for a king. He ran his hands over his shaved scalp. He had to get up. He had to. He must. There would come a day when he wouldn't get up and that would mark the beginning of the end but that day wasn't today. He couldn't let that day be today.

He swung his feet over the side of the bed and made sure that they both touched the ground at the same time.

He had to take care of himself all of the time. Couldn't afford the slightest injury. He made sure his back was straight and then he stood. Standing, he pushed his feet into his Ostrich-skin slippers.

He walked slowly and carefully towards the window, the glass curtain that fell from ceiling to floor. When he was closer it was easy to see where the sandstorms had etched the glass. The outside surface was pitted and marked. One of the huge panels that made up the window had, for some reason, started to yellow and none of the glass would now darken. The electrochromic system for the top floors had failed five years ago and David wasn't going to live any lower than where he was now.

He looked down from the window and saw the last few clouds dissolve away in the morning light. As they dispersed he saw through them to the ground, the dessert floor, almost a kilometre below.

With floor to ceiling windows that look out over the Namib Desert or the Atlantic Ocean, a Spire home is an experience like no other. A statement about yourself and the way you choose to live your life.
Palm International Real Estate. © 2024

'Come,' said Margi. 'It is time to get up.'

Zac grumbled and pulled the thin blue sleeping bag over his head. He left a bony elbow pointed out towards his mother as a defence.

'I will not tell you again. Up. You must get up. It will soon be light,' and she nudged him with the worn-out sole of her shoe. She stepped over Chen who was curled up beneath a kudu skin. It was better to let the younger boy sleep than to hear him plead to go with his brother. He was still too small.

Margi let the rag curtain that separated their sleeping corner from the rest of the shipping container fall back into place and then, on her way back to the stove, she pressed a switch and a bare light bulb began to glow with a weak, warm light. She picked her way across the floor, around piles of salvage and past heaps of scrap. Things for making a future that were also the ruins of the past. She stepped up to the container doors and released the metal bar that kept them locked shut at night. She pushed one side of the double doors open and peered out; looked left and looked right then took a step out into the pre-dawn and onto the hard-packed dirt. Margi wrapped the thin housecoat tightly around herself. The desert was bitterly cold at night, still painfully cold in the morning. Not until she felt the sun would she once again feel warm. She wondered if she should say a little prayer? Maybe a plea that this new day might be better than the ones that had gone before, but God had deserted the world. She could ask, but no God would listen. Perhaps there weren't enough people left for God to bother with, not enough voices to raise a song that would reach heaven. In disgust at what had been done, God's back was turned on her children.

'Some chai, Ma,' said Zac, and she turned to take the hot mug from his hands. English was the common language of the village but some words had leaked into it from all the other tongues. From Chinese and Spanish, Hindi and Arabic. Even Russian.

Margi smiled and gently touched his cheek. He was a good boy, when all was said and done. 'What day is today?' she asked.

'You know, Ma,' he said, and he smiled.

Margi nodded her tiny head. Her eyes sparkled like jewels set in black leather as she looked up at her son. 'It is your turn to hunt then. A warrior day,' and he could hear the pride in her voice. Margi was not just African, she was San and the Bushmen delight in the hunt.

Zac smiled back at her. 'Shall I make the pap?' he asked and Margi nodded. He went back into the container leaving Margi alone.

The village began to wake.

Another day of life for the handful of survivors, almost one hundred people who had run, walked or crawled their way here, through the desert or across the ocean. They hadn't followed a star but been drawn by the spear of God. Of course, when they had arrived here they found that God had abandoned this place as well. Her spear was sunk into the sand, its tip visible from over a hundred kilometres away, but there was no sign of God here at all. The village only existed because of The Man who lived in the spear and if God had turned her back on the world, it was surely not impossible that The Man would do the same.

And yet, Margi felt no fear. She was done with fear. Fear must look elsewhere, she thought.

She took a long, slow breath and breathed in the stink of the village. She smelled burning fires and shit, the stench of rubbish-pits and the smell of her own unwashed body, the salt-tang of the ocean and that dry, cinnamon smell of the desert.

Margi was alive. She had seen plenty of death but for now she was done with it. Death must look elsewhere, she thought.

Margi had seen her husband stabbed for the sake of a

can of corned beef, seen her daughter raped and killed but she had kept herself alive and with that life she had saved her son and the boy, Chen. She had watched the world come to an end and she had awoken from that nightmare in hell, and it had turned out to be the same hard and unforgiving world that she had lived in all her life. What was there to fear for a black woman living in the desert?

The Spire goes beyond fashion or aesthetics; it is a unique vision born from the heart of imagination brought to life by a rich partnership of creativity and expertise.

Palm International Real Estate. © 2024

David walked carefully from his bedroom and into his gymnasium. An exercise bike and a cross-trainer stood facing the window. There were other pieces of equipment but their purpose was harder to decipher; twisted metal spiders inside which David was meant to squat and lift, push and press.

He stepped out of his slippers and let the silk pyjamas fall to the floor. Naked, David's body was leanly muscled, pale and hairless. He performed a graceful dive into the long, thin swimming pool. He swam to the far end and passed his hand across a sensor. There was a deep roar that built quickly in volume and pitch. The water around David began to boil and he swam against the current that was pumped towards him from jets in the pool's end wall.

Without moving a meter further forward, David swam and swam and swam. His white, naked body sparkled in the water like a fish.

Before he was truly tired, he passed his hand across the sensor again and the pumps fell silent. Smoothly, he pulled himself out of the water and sat on the poolside and then he realised his mistake. There was a pile of towels next to where he had dropped his pyjamas, but he hadn't brought one to the pool. His feet were wet and floor was polished marble. David blinked, and then he blinked again. He bit the tip of his finger, very hard. The towels were maybe twenty meters away. He could, perhaps, walk slowly and carefully to them and if he did that he would not slip. To slip and break a bone would be to discover how long it took a man to die of thirst while he screamed or whimpered in pain. That was why David needed to be careful.

His heart in his mouth, David stood up and walked.

One.

Step.

At.

A.

Time.

Later, dried off and dressed in a white linen shirt and a black linen suit, David opened the drawer that held his watches. There were twenty-four of them, each in its own individual place. Each nestled on a setting of black baize. There were two Audemars Piguet, three IWC. He had a fondness for Patek Philippe and there were several of those in the drawer as well as a few Rolex and a big, heavy Cartier Tank. David selected one and put it on his wrist. He didn't bother to set the right time. He didn't even check to see if it was still running. What would have been the point? He shot his cuffs, adjusted his shirt collar and brushed a speck of something off the jacket's lapel. He gazed into the mirror and the mirror gazed back. David reached out to touch his reflection, to touch his cold, two-dimensional face.

In his kitchen, he went through all three of the giant

refrigerators and found very little. A couple of eggs and some tired-looking veg. He had been getting slack. He'd been forgetting things. He couldn't allow that to happen. After all, he simply had to demand what he wanted and, like a petulant child with a rich daddy, he would receive.

He would cook the eggs when he got back but what he had to do first was visit the core and send the lift down. And what was he doing by doing that, he thought? Was he foraging, or hunting? Was it farming?

It was how he lived, in any event.

The Spire fully reflects the commitment to the environment shown by the individuals and corporations that the building is designed to excite.
Even at full capacity, the Spire generates more power and water than it consumes.
Palm International Real Estate. © 2024

Zac ran through the village to the drumbeat of his heart, excited at the prospect of going on the hunt.

Originally, the villagers had taken it in turns to go out into the desert or explore along the shoreline searching for food but they quickly realised that some were more suited to the task than others and if the village was to survive, people had to do the things that they were best at. Zac could walk all day and run when he needed to. He could be quiet and he could kill. He wasn't upset when he saw jackals eating dead seal pups on the shoreline. He didn't mind when his arms were soaked to the elbow in hot blood.

A hunter he may have been, but as he ran he didn't realise that he was being followed.

The hunting party gathered on the edge of the village.

The shipping containers and patched-up site-huts, tents and shacks built of old insulation board stopped here and the empty desert began. Most of the villagers had made themselves a shelter or found shelter in something that The Fall had left standing but not everyone; some had been left too traumatised and even now, years later, there were still twenty-three people who slept in the open or sheltered in some corner of the wreckage that couldn't possibly be called a home.

Zac turned and looked back over the little village that was the world. The village was tiny compared to the tower that stood behind it. The village was a droplet of blood that ran from the tip of the spear of God. The village was the open wound at the spear's barbed head.

The sun had lit the top of the impossibly tall building over forty minutes ago and now, just now, it was starting to fall on the broad, triangular base. The bottom floors of the tower were blackened and burnt out where the fires had raged all those years ago. The skeletons of construction cranes surrounded the tower twisted by heat and writhing in their death. The landscape closer in was scarred by scorched concrete and puddles of metal where the temporary city had been that housed the workers who had been building the tower.

Before The Fall, that is.

When The Fall reached this place it had lit an inferno that consumed every person and every thing, then it lapped like a tidal wave against the base of the tower until it burned itself out at last. The first villagers had come later to find this place reeking still of death and smoke.

And they had also found The Man.

It was because of The Man that they stayed. It was

because of The Man that they had planted beds of millet, sorghum and maize, melons, wheat and tomatoes. It was because of The Man that Zac was about to go hunting.

'Hola,' he said to the group that waited for him. 'Ni hao,' to two Asian men. 'Sawubona,' to a dark face he recognised from hunting before and then he just smiled and nodded his head to the rest. Piet was leading the hunt, a skeletal white African with the devil's own luck when it came to finding game. Piet told people that before The Fall he had been a ranger and tracker but one night, when he was drunk on sorghum beer, he had bragged that the game he liked to hunt most had walked on two legs.

'Is everyone ready?' said Piet. There were nods and weapons silently raised. Piet spat on the dirt. 'Let's go.'

In single file, they walked into the desert and within a half hour they were a mile inland and the dunes began to rise around them. As they climbed, they could turn and see the ocean behind the slim, stiletto blade of the tower and they could see the scrappy mess of their village. The land around the village was grey, pink and purple. The buildings were children's toys strewn across a threadbare carpet. The dunes, by contrast, were magnificent. Smooth sweeping waves of gold and ripples of beaten bronze.

They walked until they came to a dried-up riverbed. Piet clenched his fist in the air and they came to a halt.

The floor of the canyon was covered by a low, creeping plait of tsamma melon. It was a good place to find game and almost straightaway there was a noise, a noise behind them of a small animal trying to take cover. The whole party turned and saw Chen. The boy had been following them and now he was caught between the low curve of a dune and a dried-out, scrubby patch of the vine.

'Fok, jou poes,' growled Piet. 'What you doin' here, boy?'

Chen's mouth hung slackly and he made no reply.

'Trying to be fokkin killed, eh? Is that why you are here?' Piet said and took a step forward but Zac stepped between them.

'With me,' he said. 'He's with me. It's too far to send him back alone.' Zac stood tall and bravely pushed his skinny chest out, every inch the little man.

'He's too small,' said Piet. 'I can't look out for 'im as well, eh.'

'I will,' said Zac, knowing how much it meant to Chen.

'Qing ni,' said Chen quietly, looking Piet in the eye. 'Please.'

'Stom kut,' spat Piet and shook his head, but he turned and walked away. 'Kom on you fokkers. Let's hunt, eh.'

Zac took Chen's hand, his black skin and Chen's yellow flesh intertwined. Zac looked into Chen's eyes and sighed in exasperation but he knew why the boy was here. Even in the desert, even after the end of the world, boys rush to become men. And they were brothers after all, what else could he do?

The hunting party walked on. The riverbed was covered in smooth stones. Here and there were patches of tsamma vine. The sky was cloudless and the sun burnt down but the ocean breeze kept the party cool. They walked, they watched and they waited for luck and Piet's skill to bring them what they needed.

Another hour. Zac could see Chen tiring but he didn't dare say a word. Some of the other men were looking at Chen as if he had brought them bad luck.

They walked around a bend and suddenly a piece of the

landscape didn't look like rock, sand and branch any more. It looked like gemsbok. An old female. Sad and tired.

Piet's crossbow was pointed at the ground. He looked at the man standing beside him. 'Do it,' he muttered. The man raised his arm slowly, the Oryx just watched him. He pulled the trigger and tasered the animal in the shoulder. The two darts sank through the dusty hide and delivered their electroshock. The gemsbok twisted and leaped in the air. Its back twisted so sharply that it seemed it must break its own spine. Falling to the ground, the animal convulsed twice and then lay still. One of the Chinese boys ran up to the animal and hit it in the head with his sledgehammer. The skull broke and the animal's face caved in. Its eye exploded out of the socket. A spray of brains fell over the boy's chest and he bellowed with joy. Zac ran to the dying beast, knelt by its neck and pulled his panga across its throat. The blade sliced through hide and flesh and cut into an artery. A litre of dark red blood gushed out of the wound and covered Zac's arms. He could hear the rest of the party cheering and whooping. There was blood and dust and the smell of sweat, piss and beast. He could feel Chen hug him around the head. The fallen gemsbok convulsed once again and its front hoof slammed into Chen's chest.

The young boy flew well over a meter in the air before he fell to the ground, motionless and silent.

Enter the spacious lobby with its fifteen express elevators and Italian marble floors and you have entered a world of sophistication and style.

Palm International Real Estate. © 2024

David put the boxes onto a luggage cart and pushed it out

of his penthouse and down the corridor towards the core where the lifts were.

Here at the top of The Spire, where the floor plan had narrowed down to just a few hundred meters across, the journey didn't take long. Only four lifts made it up to David's floor, the hundred and eighty fifth, and of those only one still worked. David was sure that if more of the lifts had kept on working, he would now be dead.

David pressed the button and the lift doors opened immediately. He kept it parked on this floor, just in case.

As always, when he stepped into the lift he felt fear. Try as he might, he couldn't avoid thinking of that half-a-kilometre drop; that five-hundred-metre empty shaft beneath his feet and only the thickness of the lift floor between him and falling. He slid his swipe card into the reader and the digital pad lit up. He keyed in the floor number, as far down as this lift would go, and the doors closed. The lift ran on a ratchet system, cables would have been too heavy, and it was fast but the journey down to the ninety sixth floor still took almost a minute.

He watched the floor indicator as it ticked down. The lift slowed as it approached the end of its journey.

David had been lucky. He had known just enough about The Spire to keep himself alive. He had known that none of the lifts went all the way from bottom to top and that there were "lobby floors" where that journey was split between two or more elevators. He had known about the refuge floors and how their fire suppression systems would stop the fires that had raged around the base of the tower from climbing higher than they did. He had known how to isolate himself at the top of The Spire and he had known how to make himself safe.

And when the first villagers had arrived, he had seen a way to make The Spire his fortune, as well as his fortress.

Before The Fall, David had been a billionaire, but as he had been fond of saying, that simply made him one member of a club of about three thousand. He'd owned Palm International SA. He'd been the first to move into the building to show his commitment to the project, for the PR. The day he moved in was the day the oil stopped flowing, the day the first of the power grids began to fail, the birth day of the end of the world, the first global stumble that led to The Fall.

And now David had to focus and David had to be careful.

The lift doors opened and he took a deep breath before pushing the cart out into the lobby.

The marble floor was covered in sand. One of the windows had failed and over the years tons of sand had blown in. There were black, oily stains above three of the other lift doors where smoke and flame had billowed up the shafts and out into the lobby. Another pair of doors had melted and partly fallen in but the fire control systems had been triggered and stopped the damage. The Spire had been built with the safety of its residents in mind.

David pushed the cart over to lift number sixteen. The path between the two sets of lifts was relatively free of sand. This was a journey David had often made.

This was the deal that David had made with the first villagers and, as long as no one thought about it too much, it was simple and straightforward.

The Spire made water and it made electricity. The building produced an enormous wealth of each, thousands of gallons of cool, sweet water and thousands of kilowatts of energy. David had decided that the energy and the water were his to do with as he wished.

When the first villagers arrived, he had already started to see an end to being able to survive on the food that he could find in The Spire. He also knew that he was no hunter, no farmer.

Drawn by the kilometre-high landmark, people began to arrive.

They came in ones and twos. They came in small bands and little groups that had met and clung together. They came across the desert and they came along the coast and half a dozen of them had even come by sea. Universally, they were traumatised. Parched and famished. Horrified by what they had seen and, in many cases, what they had done. The Fall had taken civilisation from the world and these survivors had seen just what people were capable of if there was no law, no rule, no consequence other than survival or death.

David, the billionaire, had offered to do what he had done with people all his life; he had offered to buy them.

He would give them water and power and they would give him food and obedience. Both parties had reacted instinctively to the deal. It was what they had been used to. It felt familiar. In the world after The Fall it felt like comfort and safety and home.

Ten years later, it was now simply how they lived. The hundred people who lived here, on the Namibian coast, in and around a tower built as a resort for the super-rich. Cut off from whatever might remain of the world's population by sand and by sea.

Isolated.

Surviving.

Continuing the very inequalities that had triggered The Fall.

From his perspective at the top of his bone-white tower, David could see that and he could see that with every day that passed the villagers were more likely to see it too and drag him from his fortress and tear him limb from limb for the injustice that he visited upon them.

Inside The Spire, office floors are located at the bottom to take advantage of larger floor plates followed by the hotel, serviced apartments, and residential units. At the very top, a massive penthouse allows one tenant to reside at the crown of the building.

Palm International Real Estate. © 2024

'Dank die Hemel daarvoor,' gasped Piet as the village came in sight. 'Thank fuck for that.'

The skinny white man had carried Chen on his back the whole way from the canyon. He wouldn't let anyone else help. His shirt was black with sweat and his scrawny brown legs trembled with every step he took.

'My responsibility, eh,' was all he said. 'My fookin' fault.' He held Chen on his back by the boy's arms, he hung there like an empty bag breathing but barely conscious.

'He was in my squad,' wheezed Piet. 'We don't leave our boys behind.'

Zac stumbled along beside them trying to be brave but his tears had washed the dust from his cheeks. His eyes were fixed and glassy.

Four men carried the half-butchered gemsbok. The head with its magnificent horns had been hacked off and its legs were tied together with wire and then slung between two spears. The hunting party threaded their way between the shacks, stepping over the cables and pipework that distributed water and power. Like veins they spread out from a cistern and junction box on the village's edge connected to the tower by an umbilicus of three-phase cabling and high-pressure fire hose.

Piet and his crew began to attract a crowd. Half a dozen children ran next to them kicking up dust; laughing and shouting as they saw the gemsbok carried in, silent when they saw Chen's small body.

'Get Margi,' said Piet.

'Get Margi,' echoed the crowd and two men ran off towards her home.

In the middle of the village was a boma, a fire pit sunk into a shallow amphitheatre and surrounded by a thornbush fence. It was where the village gathered, their communal space. It was where Piet gently laid Chen's body down. Zac stood beside them, his face blank with shock. A few minutes later Margi ran into the boma, her housecoat fluttering around her and her ancient plimsolls flapping on the dusty ground.

She knelt by Chen and for a moment, everything was still and then she howled in pain; such noise from such a tiny frame.

Piet hung his head and then, nervously, reached out to touch Margi's shoulder. 'He is not...' he began but Margi wailed all the louder. 'Bly stil,' he said. 'He is not dead. He is not dead.'

Margi still shivered as the sobs wracked her body but she became quieter. She touched Chen's cheek. 'Burning,' she whispered. 'He is on fire.'

'He's been sick, Ma,' said Zac.

She turned on him like a whip. 'I can see he is…' she snapped.

'He puked. The boy means he puked, eh,' said Piet. 'Ah, he's fookin' crook, man. I'm so sorry.'

There was a crowd of twenty or more villagers around them now. They ducked and bobbed their heads like feeding birds to get a view of what was going on but they didn't offer help or advice.

'My boy, my boy,' keened Margi stroking Chen's sallow skin.

Suddenly, Chen convulsed. He turned his head to one side and retched, a thin stream of watery bile splashed down his chin and onto his chest. His eyes fluttered and for a second he appeared to be looking straight at Margi. 'Wo bing lee. Wo bing lee,' he moaned and then his eyes closed again.

'What does he say?' said Margi looking at the crowd.

'He says he is sick,' said one of the Asian men and then dropped his gaze to the ground. 'Just that. He say that.'

'Help him,' she said.

'He is weak,' said a voice in the crowd. 'He will die.'

'No,' said Margi. 'I found him in the desert. I carried him to this place on my back. I fed him. I nursed him. Like my own son,' and she looked at Zac. 'I have lost my husband and my daughter. My brothers and sisters, all are gone. Death must leave me alone now. Death must look elsewhere.'

'There is nothing we can do,' said the voice in the crowd.

'Yes,' said Margi. 'Yes, there is,' and she turned and looked at the tower that rose out of the desert, like a spear thrown by God.

Seen from The Spire, dawn in the desert is astonishing. In the beginning the heavens and the earth are equally black. It is impossible to distinguish one from the other.

Palm International Real Estate. © 2024

David woke, and he woke as he did every morning. He woke in fear.

He kept his eyes closed as he took his first, slow breath fully conscious. He smelt no smoke and he heard no screaming. He lay still in his enormous bed and then a tremor ran through his body; like a shiver, but he wasn't cold. He opened his eyes to the darkness, stretched out one hand and found the light switch. When the lights came on, his floor-to-ceiling window became an enormous mirror in which he saw himself dwarfed by the bed, by the room, by the space he was in. Like a man buried in a giant sarcophagus a thousand metres above the earth. A specimen entombed in the sky.

When he got out of bed, David was careful that both feet touched the floor at the same time. He dare not risk a pulled muscle or a twisted back. The slightest injury could be the death of him.

There was no one to care for David, but David.

In his silk pyjamas he walked to the wet room. He passed his hand over the sensor and there was a deluge; a pre-set, temperature controlled, deluge.

Later, dried off and dressed in a white linen shirt and a black linen suit, David opened a tin of tuna for his breakfast. There was no fresh food left but it didn't matter. Yesterday he had sent the lift down to the ground floor; the villagers would fill it with food. Today he would bring the lift back up and in exchange for that food he would leave the power and water to the village turned on.

This was the deal. This was how they lived.

David looked out of the window. The sun was climbing slowly into the sky. It was easily mid-morning and the villagers would have filled the lift with food by now.

David opened one of the kitchen units and took out a small, black case. He opened it. Inside was a gun. A laser engraved custom Glock, gaudy as a child's toy.

David put the gun in his pocket and walked out of his apartment and towards the lift core.

Using his swipe card, he opened the lift doors. Stepped on to that thin plate of metal between him and the pit. The soles of his feet tingled with the thought of the emptiness beneath him.

The lift sank to the ninety-sixth floor.

David walked on the path through the windblown sand to the elevator doors and used his swipe card to call the lift from the ground. The gun felt as heavy as a stone in his pocket. He watched the floor indicator flicking over, the lift getting closer and closer. He took the gun from his pocket and thumbed off the safety as he did every single time for David was a careful man.

Eighty-four. Eighty-five. Eighty-six.

David's throat was dry and he swallowed to get some moisture back in his mouth.

Ninety-one. Ninety-two. Ninety-three.

He aimed the gun at the lift doors but then he saw that his hand was shaking and so he let it point at the ground once again.

'It's all OK,' he said to himself. 'It's OK.'

Ninety-four. Ninety-five. Ninety-six.

The lift doors opened.

'Oh, no,' said David.

Lying in the empty boxes that should have been full of food was a young Chinese boy wrapped in a filthy blanket. He seemed to be barely breathing. He had an ugly bruise on his chest. His eyes were closed and his lips had a bluish tinge.

'Oh, no,' said David and he sat down hard on the filthy lobby floor and stared at the boy in the lift.

At first, he had thought they had sent him a sacrifice, but then he realised it was much worse than that.

At the boy's feet was a piece of cardboard and written on the card in a childish but legible hand were some words.

HeLP theBoy, they said. Or we NO MoRE help u.

THE INCIDENT ON THE B4271

The two figures stood to the side of the road simply out of habit, after all there was no reason not to stand on the road itself. It was barely seven in the morning and the B4271 was quiet at the best of times; plus, the crash had made it totally impassable. Fifty feet of twisted metal and a Volvo V70 with a seriously crumpled front-end made an effective roadblock.

The two looked rather morose in the way that young men often do these days, particularly at the scene of an accident for which both are keen to avoid the blame.

The Welsh mist cleared slightly and a sheep popped up from the crumpled, red-brown bracken. Its jaw moved slowly from side to side and it watched the two as they stalked around each other, neither saying a word, one of them kicking at the road surface with his designer trainers. The other appeared to be discovering that this particular part of the Welsh countryside was still to receive mobile phone coverage.

The sheep ate some more. Two more of her flock emerged from the mist and joined her for breakfast. Along with the crunch of their teeth on the woody bracken there was a pinging sound as hot metal contracted in the chill.

'You just, you know, materialised out of like, nowhere,' said one of them.

'You were going too fast. You couldn't have been looking,' said the other.

'I was looking. I was looking at an empty road and then all of a sudden it was full of that,' and he pointed. He pointed at what had brought his Volvo to a sudden halt.

The other shook his head. 'You came over the brow of the hill too fast. You know you did.'

They glowered at each other, watched by the sheep that all seemed interested in how things might pan out.

The blond man pulled some tobacco and papers out of his trouser pocket and began to make a roll-up. Never an easy task in inclement conditions; he managed to get some twisted, lumpy little thing together and then patted his pockets before looking to the dark-haired guy. 'You got a light?' he asked.

The dark-haired figure shrugged and gestured at what he was wearing; a one-piece boiler suit with no pockets at all.

The blond pointed at the other's vehicle and raised an eyebrow.

'No,' said the other guy. 'Oddly that's something they don't come fitted with any more.'

The blond pursed his lips and slowly crumpled the roll-up between his fingers till specks of tobacco and shreds of paper lay on the wet road. The three sheep looked on at that in disapproval.

The land for miles and miles around was criss-crossed with sheep tracks and the pathways of chubby little moorland ponies but the road was a man-track, just a single black vein threading across the hilltops. Blocked.

The blond shook his head in what he obviously thought was a way that communicated his disbelief at the situation. 'You just appeared, didn't you? One second you weren't there. Then the next…Wham! You were.'

The other looked sheepish.

'It's true, isn't it? That's what happened, eh? This thing just materialised, didn't it?'

The dark-haired guy frowned. The sheep frowned. The misty landscape held its breath.

'Did it?' asked the blond. 'Can it just materialise?'

'Kind of,' said the sheepish one.

'Kind of!' squeaked the other. 'Fucking, kind of. What do you mean, kind of?'

'Well, yeah. A bit. I guess it can.'

They both turned and looked at the spaceship that the Volvo had crashed into. She was, indeed, a beautiful spaceship. Light and delicate and subtle, she seemed to tremble slightly with an energy that longed to be set free. She seemed to be alive in that machine way that great steam locomotives are but this was no steam train. Graced with swooping organic lines and a shimmering, iridescent surface. More sculpture than spacecraft, this was state-of-the-art, fifty feet long and spun into being from wisps and tendrils of silver and bronze.

'How does it even do that?' asked the earthman.

'What, materialise?' replied the spaceman. 'Well you know it just… You take it out of one mode and… It just does.'

'Hah! You don't even know how it works. No wonder you can't drive the bastard for shit. Look what you've done to my fucking car.'

'Oh right,' said the spaceman. 'And you know how that works do you?' He pointed at the Volvo. 'Which makes you mister-safe-as-houses-driving-man. You were going too bloody fast to stop.'

'To stop for what? For a fucking spaceship parked in the, you know, middle of the road which, like, the Highway Code specifically asks you to look out for at all times. I don't think so. No.'

'It's seven in the morning,' said the spaceman. 'And the only thing that's moving for miles are those bloody sheep. You were caning it down here and you weren't paying attention. You weren't looking where you were going. Simple as that.'

'And what about you, bud? For some sort of advanced alien super species you showed pretty poor decision skills in regard to where to stop, eh?'

The two men, the earthman and the spaceman, paused to take a breath. They looked at each other and shrugged. Just two guys out driving in the morning and had a bit of a bump. Shit happens. The mist was slowly clearing. As the day began to begin, they could see further and further until the first glow of morning sunlight defined a far horizon.

'There is literally nothing for miles. Nothing,' said the man, looking around. 'And we manage to bump into each other.'

'I know. It's crap, eh? Arthur's Stone is just over there though,' said the spaceman.

'What?'

'Arthur's Stone. It's just over there, about, oh I don't know, just a few hundred metres. It's famous.'

The earthman looked hard at the spaceman and then

began to slowly nod his head. He sighed. 'That's why you stopped, isn't it? You wanted to have a look at some, you know, ancient rock.'

'It's not a rock, it's a Stone, man.'

'So? So isn't there a car park or something? Surely most people don't just park in the middle of the road?'

'Well I, erm...' The dark-haired spaceman in his one-piece, pocketless overall chewed his lip and looked over at the sheep as if expecting moral support.

'Can you actually fly that fucking thing?' asked the earthman, nodding at the spaceship.

'What? No. I mean, of course I can. Well. Kind of what you actually do is punch your destination into this thing called a sat-nav, pretty cool, eh? And then the ship just takes you there. It's what they call "Driverless".'

The earthman laughed.

'I know it sounds amazing to you,' said the spaceman, 'but it's true.'

'So you're wombling along on your way to SA14 8QT or wherever and suddenly you think. 'Oh, an ancient rock! Let's stop and have a look and maybe take a bloody selfie and you slam the breaks on and... And, you know, then this.'

'Pretty much,' said the spaceman looking at his boots. Then he looked up and smiled. 'You still came over that hill fucking fast though.' And they both laughed.

'Let's go and have a look at your Stone then,' said the earthman.

'Aw, what? That's nice, man. But what about all this?' and he pointed at the spaceship and the Volvo.

'Well, I don't think anyone's going to nick it, are they? Come on. Ten minutes then we come back and decide what to do about all this shit.'

The two men walked into the remains of the mist.

The moor was a very simple landscape. No trees, no bushes. All the moor consisted of was short green grass, bracken, thin brown reeds and patches of black oily mud. The grass was as neat and closely trimmed as a golf course. As they walked, they came upon some of the tiny moorland sheep and fat-bellied ponies that kept it that way.

The ponies reminded one of the men of Thelwell cartoons from the 1970s; for the other they had no cultural significance whatsoever.

'So how come I see you this way?' asked the earthman, gesturing towards the other.

'How do you mean?'

'Well, you look just like a human. You look just like me. So I guess you're using a, you know, holographic projector or some weirdo mind-meld technique to make me…'

'Fuck off! This is what I look like.'

'Well how does that make sense?' asked the earthman. 'You look just like a…'

'A Life. That's what I look like and that's what you look like too. We are Life and so we look like this 'cos that's what Life looks like. OK?'

The earthman scratched his head. 'But shouldn't you be like super-skinny with massive great big eyes and a huge domed forehead and tiny mouth and long, spindly fingers?'

The spaceman laughed. 'That sounds like Djadit Pirson. He is one weird, ugly looking fucker, isn't he? Works in DataMining and goes out with… Oh, hang on. You aren't talking about him are you? Right. You mean like Area 51 and all that shit.'

'Yes,' said the earthman looking down at the primordial

ooze on his shoes.

'No, we are Life bro. We are what it looks like. Me and you.'

'What…everywhere?'

'Pretty much. Didn't you ever wonder how you came to be top dog on this rock? You design life-like robots and they end up being, well, Life-like. You-like. You can climb, swim, walk and run. You can exist almost anywhere on the planet. Any conditions, any place.'

'Yeah, but…'

'Strong limbs. Four of them, ending in flexible digits. Major organs on the inside of a relatively well-armoured thorax. Brain and sensory stuff inside a solid shell perched on top of the whole body. Carbon-based. Oxygen-breathing. Stereoscopic vision. Sure, you get some variety here and there but we are the basic blueprint because it works.'

'So all those old sci-fi movies where the monsters…' The spaceman frowned at the earthman. 'Sorry, I mean aliens. All the aliens looked like people but blue and with a ridge on their head…'

'Yep. They're pretty damn accurate. The Life around IC 3418 in the Virgo cluster is blue. The ridgey-head thing I'm not so sure about. Sounds weird.'

The earthman looked mildly depressed and they walked on in silence, eventually coming to Arthur's Stone, a huge chunk of pale rock balanced on top of twenty or thirty smaller stones. All around the Stone itself there were smaller rocks dotted over the ground in a spiral.

Two dirty-white moorland ponies were nibbling the tender grass from between them.

'Just like Thelwell ponies, aren't they?' said the spaceman.

The earthman looked blank and shrugged. 'How old is this then?' he asked, pointing at the stones.

'About four and a half thousand years.'

'And what's the deal? Why did you want to see it so much?'

The spaceman scratched at his chin. 'Some of the more evolved Lives, they err. Some of the more advanced cultures get a bit, what you might call, self-important. This,' he said pointing at the pile of rocks. 'This is a stage that we were all once at; we've all been through. When you see yourselves as masters of the universe, it doesn't do you any harm to remember that once upon a time you thought that banging rocks together was pretty fuckin' cool.'

'Right. Right,' said the earthman. 'Well, you've seen it now. Happy? He turned and started to retrace his steps. 'We've still got a big mess to um, you know, sort out.'

They walked back towards the road. It soon became clear that everything was not as they had left it.

Floating above the two damaged vehicles and the fascinated sheep was a huge, silver spacecraft. More than three times the size of the first ship, it had a pointed, boat-shaped hull and a pair of stubby wings with engine nacelles sculptured onto them. One section of the front had swung down to form a platform boarded with a low safety-rail. Behind the rail stood a tall, distinguished looking Life.

'Amozi Crav, I'm disappointed in you,' he said.

The earthman had already guessed this. If the guy he had met fifteen minutes ago was someone he now recognised as a spaceman then the tall figure on the balcony looking down at them was definitely a Super-man. He had grey hair in a majestic mane, regal features and perfect skin and he was arrogant-looking as fuck.

'Did you hear me, Amozi?'

'Yes, Dad.'

The earthman choked back a laugh.

'I suppose that you are expecting me to clear all this up? Am I correct in thinking that?'

The earthman turned to look at the spaceman standing next to him, who he now assumed was called Amozi. The dude looked distinctly awkward. 'Yeah,' he murmured.

The Super-man leaned a little further forward over the balcony so that he could look down on Amozi in a more obvious and patronising way. 'Pardon me,' and then he continued, 'you took the Hopper without asking. You are aware of the fact that you are not covered by the insurance, I assume.'

'Yes, Dad.'

'And you are aware of the fact that simply turning off the Driverless mode and dropping out of StealthFliteTM, I assume that is what you did, invalidates the warranty. You are also aware of that, yes?'

'Dad. Yes, Dad.'

'And what of this proto-Life? Does the other vehicle belong to it?'

'What? You said I was a Life!' said the earthman.

'Oh, not this again,' said the Super-man. 'Have you given it a name yet?'

'My name is Colin Kirkwell. I'm Colin Kirkwell. He doesn't get to give me a name. I've already got a,,,huhhhhhggh.'

A pale beam of light came down from the balcony and lit the earthman up like an electric light bulb. He glowed with a rather painful-looking luminescence and rose two or three feet off the ground. His body went rigid, head thrown back, arms out from his sides as if crucified. He trembled and the scream died in his throat.

'Oh, don't, Dad.'

'No. You have enough pets. You don't even clean their cages. I see no reason why your mother and I should look after your pets. Let this be enough, now. Perhaps you can learn.'

A pair of bay-doors opened in the hull of the floating spacecraft and tractor beams emerged to grasp the crippled spaceship and the broken Volvo. Gracefully they rose up and were swallowed into the gleaming hull.

'I refuse to bring that aboard,' said the Superman.

The spaceman opened his hands in a pleading gesture and looked up into his father's stern eyes. He just saw the older man shake his head and then press a button on the console. The field surrounding the earthman collapsed in on itself until it was just a floating orb the size of a fist. The light disappeared and a handful of fragments and offal fell to the moorland grass.

The spaceman's shoulders fell and he used the toe of his shoe to grind some of the fragments into the ooze.

'It was called Colin, Dad. It was a Colin. I haven't got a Colin.'

READY OR NOT

DEREK TOOK Sea View Cottage on a long Summer let. It didn't actually have a view of the sea but Mrs Trenoweth had read somewhere that marketing was all about telling people what they wanted to hear rather than what might actually be true so she had taken the liberty of being slightly optimistic with the property's name.

To be fair, she reckoned that if you could stand on the roof of the cottage you would get a perfectly good glimpse of the sea and if you walked no more than a hundred yards up the sandy track that led past the small garden then you would be able clearly to see the sea. In fact, just minutes' walk further on, you could see how the path would lead you down across the fields to the dunes that sat at the back of the cove.

So Sea View Cottage almost had a view of the sea and it certainly had, what they call 'easy access' to the sea. What it didn't have was wi-fi or satellite television or broadband or mobile phone reception. In fact, there was no telephone at all. No Netflix or Nespresso machine. No hot tub and no sauna. It hadn't been modernised or gentrified. It wasn't surfer-cool or family-friendly. It was an old cottage at the end of a long track and that's all it was.

If Sea View Cottage appealed to anyone, it appealed to people who wanted to get away from it all and to escape the modern world.

So it appealed to Derek a great deal.

June 2nd

He was driving an ancient short-wheelbase Land Rover.

Summer had arrived but the tourists were still weeks away so Derek had no difficulty steering the old vehicle down lanes that became increasingly narrow and between Cornish hedges that were waves of swaying grass and roadside weeds that the warm breeze had already spun into gold.

There were passing places let into the sides of the single-track lane but he didn't have to use them. There was an occasional thirty-mile-an-hour sign but he didn't feel like driving that fast. There was an old OS map on the seat next to him, folded to show this little patch of country, a church tower here and an old barrow there and a twisting line of red felt-pen showing the way to Sea View Cottage.

No sat-nav. No Google Maps.

Both windows were wound down and the choppy grunt of the diesel bounced off the confining hedges and echoed back into the cab. The diffs whined, the tyres were noisy and there were distinct rattles coming from under the bonnet. Of course, it wasn't as if she had come from an official dealer.

As he turned the next bend, he saw a sign asking people to drive carefully through the village of Porth Haeva so

Derek slowed down to a crawling twenty. He propped his elbow on the driver's door and leaned his face into his hand but there was no one about to see him and even if there were, why should they look and why should they remember?

He drove steadily past the church on his left and the pub and a Post Office stores on the right. There was a bow-fronted tearoom that had yet to open and a fish and chip shop that was still closed. Almost all the houses were small and well maintained.

Peering over the tops of his fingers, Derek paid close attention to the pub and the stores but he saw no sign of any security cameras. In a country where the population was more observed than anywhere else in Europe, this was one of the blind spots but of course, that was no accident.

The last time his face had appeared on CCTV was at a garage over a hundred miles back. The forecourt camera showed him filling the Land Rover with diesel, a camera behind the counter showed him paying and then the forecourt camera watched him as he drove away. What neither camera saw was what happened while he was waiting for the previous car to drive off so he could drive up to the pump. Derek had pulled his debit card out of his wallet and rubbed his thumb over the bottom corner where his name was embossed. He rubbed and rubbed but his name stayed there, clear and easy to read. He then bent the card in half then reluctantly snapped it in two.

Abracadabra, he thought. Disappear.

He pulled a handful of cash out of his pocket and went and paid for his fuel.

And now, a few hours later, here he was, a bland and nameless man in his late fifties wearing khaki shorts and a pale blue shirt driving a tired and dusty Defender. That was as close to invisible as you could get here on the Cornish coast. It was almost as if he were part of the landscape; like a rock, a tree or a pile of sand. The wind left deeper footprints, the tide left more of a mark.

The line on his map led out of the village for another mile and then turned to follow a single-track lane before stopping in the middle of the fields halfway between Porth Haeva the beach and Porth Haeva the village.

Derek checked his watch. He'd arranged to meet Mrs Trenoweth at the cottage at one-thirty.

'Why don't you just give me a ring when you get to the village,' she had said and Derek had replied that he didn't have a mobile phone, which wasn't true at all of course.

'I generally let the cottage by the week. Or perhaps the fortnight,' said Mrs Trenoweth. 'There'll be people looking forward to staying for their holidays this year. It seems wrong to disappoint 'em.'

Derek had mentioned a surprisingly generous weekly rental and then used the word 'cash'. Mrs Trenoweth had said that would probably do and she only had one or two regulars anyway and one of them had stayed at one of those posh places in the village last year so perhaps it would be alright as Derek seemed to have his heart set on the place and she would see him at half-past-one on Friday the second and please not to be late if it was all the same to him.

Mrs Trenoweth had put her phone down and Derek turned his mobile off and tossed it into a bin. It had been twenty quid from Tesco. He had three more of them in his bag, each one with a pay-as-you-go SIM bought with cash.

Mrs Trenoweth and her cottage were now less than a

mile away. He turned left and the road became a lane then the lane became a track. Not much changed other than the tarmac gave way to grit and sand and rough stone. It was like driving slowly off the edge of the world, which was exactly what Derek was looking to do.

The Land Rover rocked like a boat at sea over the lane's potholes and gullies and then he saw the haven he assumed was safe; his chosen port in this very particular storm.

Sea View Cottage lay like a warm, brown stone in the afternoon sun. A low building with a grey slate roof cement-washed to seal it against the rain. The cottage itself had three redbrick chimneys, three small upstairs windows and a long glazed porch that sheltered the front door. To the right, and built leaning against the cottage, was a stone barn, its shadow-black interior exposed as the big wooden doors sagged drowsily open in the heat of the day. All the paint on the woodwork was peeling away to show the archaeology of earlier colours and several glass panes in the porch were cracked but the low stone garden wall had been recently white-washed and the porch itself was a riot of colour from pots and pots of geraniums. The wrought-iron garden gate was thick and glossy with a generous layer of new, black paint. The front garden seemed to be a rectangle of faded and threadbare carpet but Derek guessed it was actually a lawn.

He parked the Land Rover in front of the gate, turned off the engine and, with a sigh, slid out from behind the steering wheel.

'I thought you'd never get here,' said Mrs Trenoweth; at least Derek assumed it was her. A big strong voice well suited to telling men what to do over the noise of farm machinery.

'Hello,' said Derek.

'I was going to ring you but, of course, you haven't got a phone. I'm sure I don't know what that's all about.'

'Well, I'm here now,' said Derek. 'It looks lovely.'

Mrs Trenoweth emerged from the porch, a solid, sun-browned woman with salt and pepper hair tied up in a bun and twinkling eyes. She asked him how the journey had been. She told him about the stores in the village and the chip shop but didn't mention the pub or the church. She gave him directions to her farmhouse and implied that she would very much rather he didn't come knocking on her door with asinine requests or ill-founded complaints.

Then Derek showed her the money. 'To be left alone', said Derek. 'To be off the books.'

Mrs Trenoweth had no problem with that. No VAT, no tax, and no invoice. That was how the economy down here worked best so she took the brick of money, dropped it into the pocket on her pinafore and thanked him. She thanked him by name. It was the name he had given her. But it wasn't his real name.

June 3rd

It was only a quarter to six when Derek woke and came downstairs to make himself a cup of tea.

The kitchen was at the back of the house. It had a smooth concrete floor, a kitchen table covered with oilcloth surrounded with half a dozen mismatched kitchen chairs. Gas cooker. Fridge. The kettle was an old, flat-bottomed thing with traces of enamel left on the handle but nowhere else. The gas burnt blue-red on the ring beneath it and there was a whistle that would announce when it was done.

It was still night-black outside and the kitchen's windows, un-curtained and un-shuttered, were made mirrors by the single burning light bulb that hung by its flex from the sloping ceiling.

Derek looked at himself in the mirror of the night.

He was bird-thin, with a beak of a nose and a tight-lipped mouth. There were wings of grey hair. He was perhaps a scholar or a professor, an intellectual at any rate.

He let his dressing gown fall open and for a moment he looked at his naked body in the reflection in the glass. A skeleton covered with a pale parchment of skin. Ribs clearer than muscles on his chest, a flat belly. His cock nestled like a baby bird in a patch of pubic hair. His legs seemed ridiculously slender.

The kettle whistled like a wolf and he closed the gown around himself, shy and timid in the night.

June 6th

Derek didn't feel comfortable with wandering far afield and so he stayed within the walls of the cottage and its garden and even there he jumped at shadows, but for the time it was OK to stay put because the Land Rover had been packed with supplies.

Aside from a pile of cash and a bag full of clothes, the Land Rover had been full of tea and sugar and marmalade and bacon and sausages and rice and pasta and tinned things and stuff in jars. It had been full of corned beef and canned frankfurters and tomato sauce and mayonnaise.

Other than the three burner phones, Derek had brought no tech at all. No laptop, no tablet and no smartphone. No Kindle and no DVD player. Which of course meant that he'd brought no entertainment, nothing to amuse him or pass the time.

Fortunately the cottage and Mrs Trenoweth had provided for that.

On three pine shelves in a corner of the living room were three-dozen books and a hand-written sign that said, 'Sea View Cottage Library. Take a book but leave one in its place.' The spines offered an eclectic mix from British Coastal Seabirds in full colour to the latest Jack Reacher novel and a thin pamphlet on Witchcraft and Wicca in Perranzubaloe Parish.

Derek pulled a book at random from the middle shelf. He made a cup of tea and sat a kitchen chair on to the step outside the front door. Settled and comfortable in the sun, he began to read Mr Weston's Good Wine by T. F. Powys.

June 9th

Derek woke up thinking that he would feel a lot more comfortable if he had more information on what was happening in the world so he walked into the village. He took a canvas shopping bag and a pocketful of cash.

His feet kicked up a swirl of dust and sand. A horsefly tried to settle on his neck but he flapped it away. The sky got in his eyes and made him squint. He could smell the Summer heat and hear the drone of fat bees.

In ten minutes, he was in the village and in the stores he picked up a basket full of shopping. It was all hideously expensive, like Waitrose prices but more so. When he got to the till, he asked the woman if he could order a couple of newspapers and did they deliver?

'Depends where you're staying,' replied the woman

behind the counter.

'Sea View Cottage.'

'Could do, I s'pose. There's an old milk churn stand at the end of the lane. The boy could drop 'em under there. Or for another pound or two I'm sure he'd put them through your door.'

'Not to worry. End of the lane is fine.'

'And what papers were you wanting?'

'Guardian and The Times, please.'

'What name is that?'

'Oh, just put "Sea View Cottage", eh.?' And behind him, Derek heard a woman's laugh.

'You're proper local already,' said Mrs Trenoweth, smiling as Derek turned around. 'Be careful who you invite through your door and never give away your true name. That's what we say around here.'

'Hello,' said Derek.

'Are you settling in?' she asked.

'Oh, yes.'

'Look after him, Marjorie,' said Mrs Trenoweth to the woman behind the counter. 'This one will be here all Summer. Won't you?' and then she said his name. Not his real name or his true name but the one she knew him by. So that was OK.

June 14th

'…ninety-eight, ninety-nine, one hundred. Here I come, ready or not.'

Derek had played hide-and-seek with his sister in the grounds of the old rectory where he had grown up, and in a way, no matter what training he had received since then, those childhood games had taught him the hardest thing about hiding; about staying un-found.

Derek had discovered that he could wriggle his way beneath the huge magnolia that grew in the front garden. It was the perfect hiding spot. His sister never found him there, but neither did he win every game. He would sit in the dark, cocooned in branches and leaves and flowers and utterly safe and he would start to think that perhaps some other place would be even safer? Perhaps there was a better option?

And so he would move to somewhere else.

And she would catch him.

Easy.

The lesson was this. People don't like to disappear; they don't like not to be noticed, to be unseen. It doesn't come easy and its hard work and you need huge amounts of patience.

So Derek thought, be patient and don't move.

June 20th

After a breakfast of tea and toast, Derek would walk down the lane to the milk churn stand and retrieve his newspapers.

He carried them back to the cottage folded up beneath his arm.

His story and the search for him might be on the front page, it might be somewhere further in or it might still not have got a mention at all. Whichever way it was, it would wait till he was sitting down in the cottage garden with a fresh cup of tea. The discipline of walking that half-mile with such potentially life-changing news tucked under his arm reminded Derek of the person he used to be. It felt good.

After he scanned the papers for any mention of himself, he settled down to do the crosswords. It seldom took him long, and that felt good too.

June 23rd

Day after day the most interesting things he found in the papers were the crosswords and the cricket scores and so Derek decided that they weren't looking for him yet, or perhaps that they were looking for him so fiercely that they had decided to keep the fact a secret.

In either event, the stores that he'd brought with him were almost gone so he had to go shopping. He had to go to a supermarket and they were better at watching their customers and recording what they did than any GCHQ spook so he threw a couple of things in the back of the Land Rover and pushed some money into his pocket. He drove slowly and carefully along the back roads to a village twenty miles away where he parked in the pub's car park before picking a taxi company from the cards stuck on the wall around the pay phone.

'What name?' asked the dispatcher.

Derek lied.

'Be there in ten minutes, Mister Pengelly,' said the dispatcher.

The taxi took him to the supermarket and he arranged with the driver to come back and pick him up at a quarter past two. He would pay in cash.

Derek squashed a battered baseball cap onto his head and put on a pair of dark sunglasses. A windcheater that was far too big for him changed his shape and a walking stick changed the way he walked. Derek was in full view of a dozen or more cameras inside and outside the shop and not one single recognisable image would ever come of it.

An hour later Derek was back at the cottage unloading the shopping from the Land Rover and it was as if he had never been away at all.

Will-o'-the-wisp, he thought. A ghost.

But someone saw him.

She saw him for the first time that night.

She saw him through the window, a pale, thin figure peering out into the night and sipping from a mug of tea. She frowned at him as if he was a burglar or a trespasser. He seemed faint to her. There was something not quite there about him, almost as if he was hiding or was caught in a lie.

June 28th

As the weeks passed Derek became more at home in his new life.

He took to weeding the tiny front garden and got dirt beneath his fingernails and bramble scratches on his wrists. He realised that he would have to water the geraniums in the porch but, in time, he began to care for them as well, deadheading them and snipping back any dead leaves. He found a book on houseplants in the cottage library and he started to take cuttings and propagate new plants. It was pleasant, bumbling work, going from plant to plant with kitchen scissors in hand and an old, straw hat to keep the sun off. His trousers got dirty at the knees and his shirts soaked up his sweat. He washed his clothes in the kitchen sink, and hung them outside to dry on the clothesline.

Transplanted, he was beginning to grow into a local.

July 4th

In the first week of July the school holidays began and things changed around Sea View Cottage.

For weeks people had been walking past Derek's front garden, but not very many and not very often. A little further down the lane was a field that Mrs Trenoweth had turned into a pay-and-display car park. Dog walkers, ramblers and twitchers drove past the cottage and into the field, obediently bought a ticket and then set off to walk a length of coastal footpath or throw a ball for Rover.

Derek watched them. At first he watched every single one, very closely. They tended to be Derek's age or more, to be thin and healthy looking. They tended to be wearing hi-tech outdoors gear that made them look like well-funded preppers. Derek watched each and every one out of the corner of his eye or stared blatantly at them, hands on hip like a farmer making sure no one scrumped his apples. Some of them ignored him and some of them gave him a wave and some, if he was sitting outside in the garden, would say, 'Hello,' or perhaps, 'Lovely day,' and after a time Derek accepted their presence and it no longer troubled him.

But with the school holidays the trickle turned into a torrent.

All morning a conveyor belt of people ran past his garden gate. Like targets in a shooting gallery they moved from right to left in a steady and regular flow heading from the car park to the beach.

Unlike the survival-ready, this new horde spanned the

ages from mewling infant to toothless crone. They tended to the plus-size and were either deathly white or bright red but definitely tattooed; as far as Derek could see they were all tattooed. They carried windbreaks made of nylon and surfboards made from polystyrene, buckets and fishing nets, barbecues and spades. They smiled and nodded and commented on the weather or Derek's blossoming garden. Then there was a mid-day lull before, from about five o'clock, the machine reversed itself and they returned to the car park and then drove away.

And that's when he first saw her.

Through the gaps in the crowd as it passed.

She looked like honey and milk, that's what he thought. Like something you wanted to taste on your lips or with the tip of your tongue. She looked like you'd want to lick your fingers after touching her. She was stationary and silent, watching him. Her hair curled around her face and fell over her shoulders. He could almost feel his pupils dilate as he looked into her eyes.

Then he was embarrassed and looked away.

And when he looked back, she was gone. There was an empty space where she had been. A lack of her. An absence. He looked up and down the lane but she was nowhere to be seen.

He would have called out her name if he'd known it.

July 5th

It was in the moments immediately either side of sleep that Derek felt the loneliest.

He would take himself off to bed and slip naked beneath the cheap duvet. The nights were warm so he had no need for thick blankets but something with some weight pressing against his body might have given him the feeling that another human being was in the bed with him. Loneliness is just a lack of touch and a lack of contact. As he fell into sleep, he could believe that even a cuddled pillow or a snuggled duvet was another warm soul sharing the night with him but it wasn't to be, he was a solitary soul embarked on night's journey.

Alone, he crossed over from one day to the next.

But in the morning, every morning, there was always a brief instant when he found himself awake and untroubled, a new man facing a new day. Then yesterday's fears would lay claim to the moment and poison it. A visceral emotion that made him tremble, that pulled regret and sorrow across his face like a hand clenched inside a glove puppet.

So he had learnt just to lie there and breathe.

The room slowly became lighter. There were curtains in Derek's bedroom but they were as thin as hope. Breathe. He couldn't push the dream away for that would need him to focus on it, to see it more clearly so he looked elsewhere. He rubbed his thumbs and fingers together, feeling his own solid reality. Breathe. He stretched his legs until his toes escaped the duvet and he pushed the covers half way down his chest. Breathe. Soon he could get up, sink into the shawl of his dressing gown and descend the thin, wooden staircase to the kitchen where he could make tea.

Until then, breathe.

July 15th

The crowds of tourists were now so dense that Derek felt perfectly happy to be out and amongst them, a tree hiding in the forest.

He avoided 'rush hour', both the morning one and its early-evening mirror image, but during the afternoon most people who wanted to be on the beach were on it and so the lane and the coastal path were reasonably quiet.

It felt good to stretch his legs, to step out along the pathways, to be moving after so much time spent sitting and waiting, being stationary in the hope that was the best course of action. He was under the magnolia on the rectory lawn and the urge to step out from beneath it in the search of somewhere safer was almost impossible to resist, but at least with these walks he could blow off some steam.

He walked the coastal footpath. It was bone dry and almost slippery with gravel and fine, wind-blown sand. Through a kissing gate of blackened four-by-four timber and past a noticeboard that told people what birds and plants they might expect to see and reminded them to take their dog poop home with them. The fields on either side ended and were replaced by downs; tightly cropped grass, wild flowers and weeds woven through with poppies, their red blooms like blood spatter at a crime scene.

Derek walked on. He felt the sun on his back and a warm breeze buffeting him. Terns and gulls rolled and swooped in its currents. He saw the sea and watched long waves roll in across the bay before tripping and breaking in the shallows. From up here on the cliff, the holidaymakers on the beach looked like coloured marbles thrown across a sandpit. On the downs above the cliffs on the far side of the bay a flock of sheep appeared to be playing chicken with the cliff edge.

'Hello', said a voice. 'It is you, isn't it?'

And Derek's world ended.

His heart felt as if it had stopped. A splash of bile rose in his throat. His face became slack and expressionless. His body burned and then his heart started again and the blood pounded in his veins. He was flooded with adrenaline but neither fight nor flight was a realistic option.

He slowly turned around.

'Are you OK?' asked the voice. 'You look like you've seen a ghost.'

Derek focused at last on the man who had come silently up behind him. Older. Dressed for the outdoors. He had binoculars around his neck and a smile on his lean, tanned face.

'Perhaps you should sit for a minute,' said the man.

Derek swallowed the vomit in his throat. 'I'm alright,' he said. 'You just took me by surprise.'

'I'm sorry. It is a peaceful spot, isn't it?'

Derek nodded.

'You're the man from Sea View Cottage. You've been here since the very beginning of Summer. I've seen you in your garden. You haven't bought the place, have you?'

Derek chuckled and shook his head. 'No. You don't seem to think it would be a good investment.'

'Well no one local would buy it, certainly.'

Derek rubbed at the stubble on his chin, felt his pulse slow down to something more normal. 'Built over a mine shaft, is it? I'm sure it would tidy up.'

'It's not that, it's just not a very lucky house. That's why it's a holiday let. If you're just staying in it for a week or two it's probably OK but anyone who's been there any longer has…' And the man made a little grimace as he realised what he had just said. Derek looked puzzled.

'I best let you get on,' said the rambler.

'So what makes the house unlucky then?'

'Just old wives' tales, you know how it is. Probably nothing. Almost certainly nothing.' He smiled at Derek, wished him a good day, turned on his heel and walked away.

Derek watched him go. He was annoyed, annoyed that he'd reacted so badly when he thought he had been recognised, annoyed about all the nonsense about the cottage. Frowning, he stomped back down the dry and dusty lane like a whirlwind, like a tiny cyclone; his eyes fixed to the ground once again.

'Enjoy your walk, my lover?' in a voice warm and smooth as a belly, as self-assured as a well-rounded hip. He looked up and there she was. Standing in the hedgerow just before the kissing gate. She was all curves and curls, honey and earth.

'Did you?' she asked again with a twinkle and then she laughed.

She laughed and it was the sound of the bells on Lady Godiva's toes. It was the sound of a furrow being turned ready for the seed. It was the sound of a baby, mouth full of milk and nipple.

Flustered, he stumbled past her, through the gate and almost ran for home.

July 16th

Derek awoke to the sound of the rain drowning the sea.

Rather than the ocean's bass rumble, the rain was all high notes. It was brushes on cymbals, hi-hats and a tambourine. It hissed and skittered across the glass roof of the porch, scratched against the window when the wind blew it that way and beat on the roof as if it were a tight-skinned snare.

White noise.

The room was cooler and Derek pulled the duvet tight around him. That was when he realised that his cock was as hard as a bone. Breathe. With the breath came the faint memory of the dream. She had been wet and glossy, smooth and writhing and entwining and her eyes gazing into his and... Breathe.

Derek swung his legs out of bed and his feet grounded themselves on the shabby carpet runner. He pulled the duvet into his lap to cover himself up. Looked at the thinly curtained window almost expecting to see her face there. Breathe.

The rain's cold shower drummed and hissed.

And breathe.

As the memory of the dream faded, part of him went running back through time desperate to see her again and much more painfully, desperate for her to see him. When he realised she was gone a tiny moan escaped his tight, thin lips. He slipped into his dressing gown and padded barefoot down the rough, wooden stairs. He made a cup of tea, which he drank looking out from the porch at the heavy grey skies and the downpour. The newspapers would have to wait. Perhaps they would turn into a sodden mess, perhaps they would stay dry enough but Derek was in no mind to go and find out.

By mid-morning a dribble of holidaymakers had arrived. Come hell or high water, they were going to spend the day on the beach. They looked much as they looked on every other day but had taken the precaution of shrink-wrapping themselves in see-through rainproofs, as you might preserve a sandwich by covering it in cling film. Protected against the elements, they filed past Derek's garden gate in a steady, resolute stream.

For his lunch Derek toasted a couple of slices of stale bread and opened a tin of sardines. He felt more trapped inside the house by the rain than he had felt trapped by the thought of watchers, spooks and spies. He made himself comfortable in a chair in the porch and read from the library as the rain streamed in a water-curtain from the overtaxed gutters.

Every few minutes he would look up to see if she was there.

He couldn't settle to his book. He made cups of tea that he didn't want and didn't drink. He looked in the store cupboard to see what he might have for his supper. He chose another book to read but it was no better than the first.

In late afternoon the first holidaymakers started to return from the beach. Soaked to the skin by rain and by sea, they had mostly abandoned their waterproofing and walked past as a sopping, bedraggled mass but they had got the job done. They had spent the day on the beach.

As the sun sank in the sky, the rain began to dry up. The dull and uniformly grey clouds broke up into something much more dramatic. Rolling banks of darkness with shafts of sunshine breaking between them. The sun was hidden but fingers of her light stabbed down into the earth.

Derek watched from the porch. He'd seen many remarkable evening skies here but this truly was spectacular. Sweeping the skirts of his dressing gown around him, he climbed the stairs and stood at the hall window, the middle of the upper three. From here he could see out over the lane and into the landscape where the light and shade from the heavens painted hedges and fields with ebony and gold. It was a bravura performance, a tour de force, a son et lumière; but without the son.

And then she was there.

'Fuck', said Derek out loud.

She was walking along the lane, her hips swaying with a regular, gentle pace. Her dark hair falling in curls around her face, she kept her eyes down but her head swung from side to side, oblivious to the world or simply un-concerned for it. In a long, white cotton skirt and embroidered white cotton blouse, in leather sandals and carrying a hessian bag, she could have stepped out of the distant past or out of a Range Rover in Chelsea.

'Fuck', said Derek, quietly. The tip of his tongue moistened his dry lips.

She had bare shoulders that were golden brown and bare arms, long and lean. The path was wet from the rain and her feet and the hem of her skirt were splashed with mud.

Then she saw him watching her. She didn't look for him she just looked straight at him. Her head swung from side to side in rhythm with her footsteps and then just continued rolling upwards on the strong column of her neck until her throat was taut and she was looking Derek straight in the eye. She flicked a mop of tumbling curls from her face and smiled at him.

For a brief instant, Derek thought 'honey trap', before dismissing the idea out of hand. If they knew where he was there would be helicopters and flashing lights, police cars and sirens or possibly just one faint and shady man walking up the drive with a length of wire in one gloved hand. Not a beautiful woman smiling at him from the lane. Not that.

So he smiled back.

She nodded her head, acknowledging him, and her smile turned into a pout, her lips full and wet. Her cheek dimpled and then with the slightest of gestures, she invited him down. A little 'come along' twitch with her fingers and she went to stand by the garden gate.

Derek was half-way down the stairs before he even thought, 'should I or shouldn't I?' He was still pondering the same question when he opened the door into the porch and then stepped out into the garden.

'Hello,' he said.

'Hello, my lover.'

Derek smiled.

'It's a pretty cottage, isn't it?' she said.

Derek had never ever considered the cottage to be pretty but of course he said yes, it was. And smiled.

'It was mine once, you know. In a way.'

'Mrs Trenoweth, umm… She was the lady I rented…'

'Long before her,' laughed the woman.

'Oh. Well, you don't look… That's to say that you must be much younger than Mrs Trenoweth.' And he frowned.

'That's nice of you to say, although I can't say I know just how old she is.'

Standing this close to her, Derek found the woman intoxicating. He could smell a warm, sweet musk, which he guessed must be her. Her skin had an oily, glossy sheen. Her eyes sparkled, they actually did. Brown flecked with gold and graced with huge, black pupils. Her lips were un-painted but flushed with red. As far as Derek could tell she wore no makeup at all. She wore no bra either. Through the cotton of her blouse he could see the smudges of darker brown and the raised mark her nipples made where they pressed against the cloth. He snapped his eyes back to hers and he swore he saw her lips twitch with amusement as lechery and politeness fought for control. The most natural thing in the world would have been to introduce himself, but he couldn't.

The two words that were his name were locked deep in his stomach and he simply couldn't spit them out. It was a visceral thing.

'May I come in?' she said, her hands gripping the top rail of the garden gate. 'It'd be nice to touch those stones again.'

'Umm. Well, I'm not really… That is, err…'

Her pink tongue slid out from between her lips and she teased her upper lip, painting a gloss on the skin. Her hand came up and cupped her breast and she squeezed. When she took her hand away, her nipple was hard and prominent.

'Invite me in,' she said. But she said it with such need that Derek took a step back and then from down the lane came the shriek of children and the gruff cry of a father and a mother's laughter and noise and commotion and life. The woman's eyes flashed with amusement and then she grinned as wide as wide could be.

'Soon, my lover,' she said. 'You need to come and join me. I'll keep you safe. Soon, you'll see.'

And she laughed. She laughed and it was the sound of a woman bathing in a stream. It was the sound of ripe corn swaying in the wind. It was the sound of kisses given gladly.

And then she turned and walked away once again, and Derek watched.

July 17th

He walked to Mrs Trenoweth's farm. He could as soon have got the Land Rover out of the shed and driven it as he could have flagged down a passing spaceship and asked for a lift.

He had stripped away all the layers that had previously made him what he had been and now he was becoming a different person, and that journey was almost done. Reduced to his core, his essence. Distilled down to just the very basics of what made him what he was, he found that spirit wasn't what he had expected at all. Gone were his cleverness, his skill and intellect. Gone his analytical mind and stiff moral compass. Those things had evaporated. He had thought they were what made him, but it turned out not.

He was flesh and blood, desire and need, longing and desperation. He was lost, and he loved it.

Derek walked through the farm gate, up the drive and into the yard. There were stone barns on two sides of the yard and a big, open timber-framed barn on the other. The farmhouse made up the fourth side. The stone buildings looked to be hundreds of years old but they all had new roofs and double-glazing. Their paint was bright and fresh.

The door to the farmhouse opened and Mrs Trenoweth came out, drying her hands on a tea towel.

'Hello,' she said, but she didn't call him by the name he had given her because he didn't quite look like that person anymore. 'Nothing's wrong is it? Everything alright at the cottage, me ansum?'

'No. Everything's fine.'

'Only I'm just about to go into town, so...?'

'How long have you had the place?' he asked.

Mrs Trenoweth twitched in surprise. Her eyebrows flew up and then fell back down again. 'Oh, my lord, as long as I can remember. Been in our family as long as we've had this farm, I think.'

'And that's?'

'Generations, my dear. Generations. Why?'

'I met someone who said that she used to live there.'

Mrs Trenoweth shrugged. 'We might have had tenants in there in the sixties but…'

'She wasn't that old.'

'Just someone having a laugh with you then. No one local would ever live there.' And Mrs Trenoweth blinked as if she had just realised what she had said.

'What do you mean?'

'Nothing.'

'No. Tell me.'

'Just stupid stories.'

'Like?'

She slapped at her leg with the tea towel. Annoyed. 'They say the cottage were built with stones taken from Havalah's barrow.'

Derek looked perplexed.

'Havalah was a witch, least that's what they say. She cared for folk around here and when she died they built a barrow for her.'

'Like a tomb?'

'A grave and a monument, that's what a barrow is. And that was all well and good 'till someone came along and, well, you know how people don't like waste, how they like to make one thing out of another. Well, some newcomer wanted to build a cottage and he decided that there was a nice big supply of stone right there and waiting so he took the barrow apart and built his cottage with it.'

'What happened?' Derek asked.

'Does it look a lucky house to you? Do you see a happy farmer and his fat wife standing in that doorway? Or perhaps their sons and daughters, three generations on?'

'No.'

'No. And nor you will 'cos it didn't turn out well for them and people say it's because Havalah's name and her resting place were lost and she didn't like that at all. That's why we say that it's unlucky to invite people in to your house that you don't know…'

'And never tell anyone your true name,' finished Derek.

Mrs Trenoweth nodded. 'But it's a fairy story, she said. 'And now I have to get to Morrisons, so I really must be off. Have a nice day.'

July 19th

Derek listened to the stumbling, choppy sound of a broken clock.

Tick tock, tock. Tock, tick. Tock.

After almost the whole Summer here he knew what it was, a bird beating a snail against a rock.

Fat bees bumbled from blossom to blossom in the porch.

Crickets made noise in the tall, dry grass growing out of the garden wall.

It had been a scorching day and it was drowsily rolling over into a warm and musty evening. Derek was waiting, again. He was stationary, again. The store cupboard was almost bare but that didn't really matter. He had showered and shaved. He thought that was polite. He felt sad, the sadness of coming to the end of a book that you have really enjoyed. The sadness of saying farewell to all those characters and places. Story's end.

But perhaps a new story was beginning, or not? It didn't bother him very much.

He pulled a chair from the kitchen and sat it in the porch doorway; on the threshold. Closed his eyes. Felt the sun on his skin. Breathed in the smell of the summer.

Breathe.

'My lovely,' she said.

He opened his eyes and she was there. Standing at the garden gate just as she had stood before but this time she had flowers in her hair, blooms from the roadside. She had a poppy in her hand. She held its blood-red splash out towards him.

'Come in,' he said. 'Come in.'

She breathed deeply and closed her eyes, pushed against the garden gate and as it swung open her eyes opened wide in delight. She bit down on her lip as she took the first step onto the short garden path, another and then another. Derek stood up and moved the chair out of the way. He stepped back into the porch and she followed him. Another threshold crossed.

She took a step past him and pressed her hand against the cottage's stonewall. Her fingers spread, her palm feeling the warmth in the stones. She closed her eyes and breathed in. Breathe.

'Thank you,' she said, opening her eyes again and looking at Derek. 'Why are you hiding?'

'Because I don't want to be found.'

'I can hide you. You could hide with me.'

'I know.'

'Someone's told you then. Told you my tale.'

'Perhaps.'

'You know my name?'

'Perhaps.'

'Tell me yours.'

And he did. His true name. Spoken aloud. Freely given.

The sound of the words hung in the air along with the bees, the crickets and the birds; the sound of their breathing, the beat of their hearts and somewhere, the roar of the sea.

She smiled as if to say, thank you, and then she spoke his name in turn.

It was as if a sparkling, spinning, shinning lure glittered in the air just before his face. His soul, delighted at being so deliciously tempted, leapt from his mouth and swallowed the bait whole. But the lure had barbs. The barbs pierced his cheek and then his throat and then his gut. As he swallowed the enticement it devoured him in good order, it hooked him and snared him and the line went tight and she pulled him towards her and she smiled like a young girl who has tickled an old trout. His mouth and eyes opened wide in horror and delight. She chuckled; the old tricks were always the best. They could never resist the lure that there might be a safer place. She kissed him full on his open mouth and breathed in and, whereas Summer could be warm and dry and pleasurable, too much of it could be drought and desiccation and desert. She sucked on him and swallowed. For a second he was hard, rigid, and then he collapsed into sand and dust that fell to the floor and motes of nothingness that hung steady in the breezeless air.

Havalah groaned, earthy and deep.

She bent down and picked up his clothes, shirt and trousers, socks but no pants. She laughed. Men were always the same, weren't they? She began carefully to fold the clothes and made a little pile of them on the kitchen table.

She walked amongst the stones that had been hers. Her barrow, raised up and reformed, surrounded her again. And now she had a companion.

She would like living here again.

August 20th

Sergeant Penrose was there to do the driving and act as local liaison but there was no doubt that Peter Chatterton-Drew was in charge, he had a GCHQ identity card to prove it.

'We'll go straight to the cottage please, Sergeant.'

'OK, sir,' said Penrose.

The unmarked Audi A6 drove slowly through the village. The sat-nav steered them out of the village and then took them left down a single-track road. On the corner was a stone milk-churn stand with a big pile of newspapers stuffed underneath it. Penrose grumbled to himself as he drove past it.

The big car glided over the ruts and potholes in the lane and came to a stop outside the cottage. 'Your destination is on your right,' said the sat-nav before Penrose killed it.

'How did you find him, if I can ask?' said Penrose.

'That's rather the point, isn't it?' said the older man. 'We haven't found him. We found where he was, but he isn't here. The bloody rabbit is no longer in the hat.'

The two men looked out at the cottage; a low building with a cement-washed, slate roof and a glass porch that seemed to be full of dead flowers. The front door was in broken fragments where the armed-response team had hit it with a hundred-pound battering ram. A policeman was standing in the garden, safe behind a line of yellow-and-black tape.

'We had a bit of luck, actually,' continued Chatterton-Drew. 'Pure bloody luck.'

Penrose turned off the engine. The older man looked at him.

'Local boys, you know, you lot, booked a dodgy car dealer in Romford on a coke bust and he started to try and bargain his way out of jail. One of the things he gave up was a Land Rover that he'd sold for cash to an individual who was keen to avoid any paperwork. He had a picture of him from the CCTV in the garage and it was our man.'

'What was his actual name?' asked Penrose.

'I'm not at liberty to answer that,' said the spook. 'We traced the car to the West Country with an ANPR search. Put his face up all over social media down here and let people believe he was a paedo. Some girl in Sainsbury's reckoned she'd served him. Remembered him because he'd paid in cash.'

'Clever', said Penrose.

'Not clever enough though,' said the older man, looking at the empty cottage. 'Come on, let's go and have a look,' and he got out of the car.

'Down here at this time of year and using cash, it was a safe bet he was in a holiday let, so then it was just down to knocking on doors. We talked to the Trenoweth woman on Tuesday I think it was. Raided the place yesterday. Helicopters and flashing lights, squad cars and sniper teams, the lot.' Chatterton-Drew pulled a pair of leather gloves out of his pocket and slipped them on. 'But the little cunt wasn't here.'

They stepped into the porch and looked around.

'What had he done?' asked Penrose. 'Why were you after him?'

'I'm not at liberty to answer that,' said the older man. 'We found a bag of cash and three pay-as-you-go phones. The Land Rover's been taken away for forensics. His prints are all over the place, but he isn't here.' Peter shook his head and then rubbed at his face with his hands. 'We knew he was good, but how did he just disappear? Vanished. Abracadabra, gone. From here, eh. It's like he stepped off the earth.'

Penrose rubbed his foot through a pile of sand and dust on the porch floor. 'Wasn't exactly house proud, was he? What happens now?'

The older man looked down at the pile. 'I keep on looking,' he said. He spat into the dust. 'Here I come. Ready or not,' and, playing with a length of thin wire, he walked out of the porch and back towards the car.

11:08:2018

MEMORIA

'MEMENTO MORI.' Remember that we die. But remember that we live as well. *'Memento vivimus.'* The common thread here is to remember.

Remember me.

We are our memories and our memories are us. Inextricable. Indivisible.

Memory is what makes us unique and individual. Only when we forget or are forgotten do we cease to be.

.

A Young Man, strong and proud and supple, came to the thought that everything that happened to him in his life would have value, that every experience should be treasured and protected, that every memory would be precious. With the energy and enthusiasm of youth he began to build a palace for his memories, a place to keep them safe and also a system of cataloguing them such as might be found in a great library. The endeavour proved so fruitful that, by the time he had grown up to be a Man, what he had raised was truly his Palace of Memories. As he lived and learned so each new experience and each new piece of knowledge came to take its place amongst the rest.

He had imagined his palace built on dry grassland between the shore and the forested slopes of the mountains. The shingle beach welcomed the low, slow waves as they softly broke upon the shore. Rising from the dense forest, the mountains looked like nothing more than clouds, pale blue, grey and purple shapes that seemed so insubstantial their roots couldn't possibly lie in the earth. The man believed that being between the sea and these peaks that scraped the sky would be good Feng Shui, and so it proved.

As the Man's life had been rich and varied, so the palace was a celebration of that. In shape and form, in material and fabric, the building reflected decades and decades of growth and change, from the monolithic masonry that formed the Always Keep to the delicate stone pillar of A Spire of Dreams. Behind the unbreachable Walls of Experience were courtyards and cloisters that were dedicated to all of the Man's interests and passions. There were galleries and walkways that led from one structure to the next tying the whole into the web of a life which sheltered beneath a tumble of roofs. Roofs of tile, of slate and stone, roofs pitched to throw off snow that never fell and rain that never dropped. Roofs that eventually leaked up into the sky in a tracery of chimneys, towers and spires.

The Man visited his palace every single day. Sometimes he came looking for the answer to a question, sometimes to relive an old pleasure or revisit an earlier sin. Everything he had ever learnt and everything he had ever experienced was here, catalogued and filed away, complete in every nuance and detail.

.

It had taken a lifetime to build but now the palace was under attack, although the Man didn't know that yet.

The Man was now of a certain age, his hair had thinned and was cut short, tipped with grey and winter-white. His beard was more salt than pepper. His eyes were still clear and his handshake still strong. His shoulders and arms were hefty and his legs muscled. He breathed easily and although he seldom laughed, he smiled at many things that he came across during his days. The Man was content, content within his palace and content within himself. He sat in his great chair, which sat on a great terrace and looked out across the bay. The Terrace of Sights.

The chair was black oak, heavily carved in the style of the early 1500s and known as a 'Glastonbury chair'. Glastonbury Tor was in Somerset but Tor was also a name for the dark web where layered routing enabled anonymous web browsing and Internet communication. The chair was furniture and a mnemonic, a place to rest and an aide-memoire. Carved into the dark oak seat was a spider and at the tip of each of its eight legs was a ten-digit number that was the IP address of one of the Man's dark-web properties. 46.208.98.197 was an Ethereum mine. 99.470.22.368 hosted encrypted fin-tech. He had a call scheduled regarding the fin-tech business tomorrow. What time, he wondered? He looked to the table at his side where his journal sat but the page for tomorrow was a blank, a plain white and pristine page. The date itself was printed clearly but there was no other mark at all.

Perhaps the appointment is yet to be made, thought the Man. And yet...

The Man stood and walked to the edge of the terrace, rested his hands on the balustrade and leant out into space to peer more closely at what he thought he had seen but the distance was too great or the object too small. A telescope leant against the rail and through that he saw the something that was being dashed to and fro by the low surf on the beach. He saw the way it flopped lifelessly from side to side as the surf threw it up the shingle and then dragged it back down to the sea. He saw how the yellow beak was shut; the round black eye was open. He saw it roll over and over in the water, a dead White Crane. That was wrong in so many ways.

The Man rubbed the palms of his hands together and listened to the sound of skin sliding against skin. He kissed the tips of his fingers. Opened his palms to make a pocket and breathed into the gap. All these things seemed exactly as they should be and yet, the White Crane should not be dead.

He went back to the table and casually flicked over a few pages of the journal. He did it in a nonchalant way that showed that this was not important, just a man riffling through pages, nothing of note. The other pages were full, or at least contained everything they might be expected to contain, appointments, meetings and such like. What he had done yesterday and what he was planning to do in a few days' time. It was only tomorrow that was blank.

The Man stared at the blank page for a while. It was as if it was challenging him in some way and he was refusing to be cowed or to back down. At last he carefully tore the page from the book and began to fold it delicately and precisely. He worked on the paper for fully five minutes.

When at last he walked away from his chair and off the

terrace he left the folded Origami figure of a Crane sitting on the seat of the chair.

.

Time passed as time does. The man visited his palace and spent time with his memories. He walked its halls with a confident tread. He spent time in the Gallery of Impressions. He climbed the ladder up to Lofty Intentions. The maze of rooms that made up the palace was as familiar to him as his own face in the mirror; he was as comfortable here as in his own skin. His boot heels clicked on the stone floors and clacked on the oaken ones. His coat tails streamed behind him. He flowed through the corridors like smoke, up a wooden staircase, down a flight of stone steps, across the sprung floor of a ballroom, through the moist greenery of an orangery. He visited moments from his childhood. He sat back down in lecture halls from his university days. He bathed in the confidence that he had enjoyed at the start of his career and soaked in the wisdom that the more recent decades had brought him. He studied again the art that he had once seen and the views he had once enjoyed. He moved through the rooms of his memory with commitment and purpose. Take the third door on the left and then second on the right.

The man came to a tall, panelled door of honeyed oak. He threw it open and stepped out into a high-ceilinged, square room. The room was lit by candlelight. The tallow flames danced their reflections across a hundred glass domes and under each dome was an animal which was as still as a statue. Taxidermy. Birds, cats, rabbits and mice; kittens, fox cubs and dogs, each and every one of them frozen in some parable of human life.

The Man looked around. He moistened his lips. The flickering candlelight seemed to animate the creatures, turned their lack of life into merely a lack of movement. He walked around a few of the exhibits, touched some of the glass domes. Slowly a frown settled across his face, a frown that deepened.

He had absolutely no idea why he had come into this room. He felt that he entered with a purpose, but he now had no idea as to what that purpose might have been.

The Man turned on his heel and marched out of the room.

He strode through the palace to his terrace and his favourite chair.

He picked the folded Crane off the chair seat and walked with it to the terrace edge. He held the paper bird in the palm of his hand. He breathed on it. 'Save me,' he said with the warmth of his breath and he threw the bird into the air.

Perhaps a thermal caught it or there was a gust of wind but for whatever reason the Crane flew into the air and out towards the inland sea.

.

New pages were turned in the journal. Many of them held notes and jottings but sometimes there came a day that was surprisingly blank, just every now and then.

Today the Man wrapped his long black cloak around his broad shoulders and stepped out onto the Terrace of Sights. He had missed dawn but the new day was still only just cast from the mould. The virgin-white gleam of sunrise was tinted the palest of yellow. Yellow is the colour of creativity, thought the Man. The red that first bled into the morning sky was the colour of birth. Blue is known for wisdom and the green means knowledge.

He looked out towards the water and there, drawn up on the shingle so that it was safely above the waves was a small wooden boat.

Someone's rowed their boat ashore, thought the Man.

Walking to the opposite end of the terrace, he looked out over the grasslands that lay between the palace and the forest. The tall grass swayed like waves in a breeze and across it, like the wake of a boat, the Man could see two tracks that led from there to here, from wood to palace. More visitors. When would the three arrive? The two from the forest and the one from the sea.

The Man sat in the Glastonbury chair.

Glastonbury Tor was in Somerset but Tor was also a name for the dark web where layered routing enabled anonymous web browsing and Internet communication.

Had he thought those self-same words before? Perhaps he had.

He crossed his ankles and closed his eyes.

After a time he heard the doors behind him open and the sound of boot-heels and claws crossing the terrace towards him.

'Thank you for coming,' said the Man, without opening his eyes.

'I'm sorry, but we cannot save you,' a voice replied.

'Perhaps you can.'

'We cannot. No one can.'

'I ask you to try', said the Man. 'This palace has taken me a lifetime to build,' and he opened his eyes and saw that, standing on the Terrace of Sights was a stranger and behind him, two wolves.

'My name is Hench,' said the stranger. 'And this is Tooth and this is Claw,' and he looked at each beast in turn.

Hench was slim and brown, he wore waxed cotton trousers and soft leather boots and the Man could tell from the casual way that he held himself that he was quick as spite and as strong as love. The two wolves had thick coats the colour of seasoned timber and eyes that sparkled like angry honey.

.

From that moment on, whenever the Man visited his memory palace either Hench or Tooth or Claw was with him; sometimes just one of them, sometimes two and sometimes all three. If truth were told, the Man felt most protected in the company of the wolves but Hench was by far the better conversationalist.

'It happened again?' said Hench.

'Yes,' said the Man. 'I was in the Cinema of Paradise and I couldn't for the life of me remember what I had gone there to see.'

'That happens to all of us,' said Hench. 'Step through a door into a new space and your brain re-sets. You think, what am I doing here? We all do.'

'Not me, I won't let that happen to me.'

'We forget. We fail to remember. We suffer from memory loss and forgetfulness.'

'I don't want that to happen. What can I do?' asked The Man.

'Take fish oil and turmeric. Grow Ginkgo Biloba and

make a paste from the leaves…'

'I don't want to eat leaves. I want you to fight for me. I want you to keep me safe.'

Hench looked at the Man. He held out his right hand. The fingers closed into a fist and the fist became a stone. He straightened his fingers and they formed a blade. 'What I can fight, I can kill,' said Hench.

'Then I'm OK,' said the Man, choosing to misunderstand what had been said.

.

More journal pages turn and more days become months and move towards years. Sand flows out of the glass.

On the northern side of the Keep was a high-ceilinged room dominated by a large, stone fireplace. A massive hearth protruded out into the room and lay level with the oak floorboards. Next to the fireplace, actually on the hearthstone, sat a wingback chair upholstered in a rich golden cloth and in the chair sat the Man, his feet pushed towards the last few flames that flickered above the grey ash in the grate. The Man held his left hand in his right and rubbed slowly and steadily at its back as if he was trying to erase a spot or smear that wasn't there.

By the side of his chair lay Claw. The wolf's big head was up. Her golden eyes were unblinking and her ears were pricked. Wine-red drapes hung at the sides of the lead-paned windows. The sky outside was heartless and grey. On the oak floor were carpets and rugs from Afghanistan and Persia. Into each detail of their design was woven a memory. Facing the window was a roll-top writing desk that seemed to explode with paper and parchment, notes and jottings. They burst from each veneered drawer, curled out from under the blotter and were wedged into an inkwell and a jam jar that held quills.

Hench walked into the Room of Living. Tooth padded behind him.

'I've been looking for a reason,' said the Man, nodding at the bureau.

'There is no reason,' said Hench.

'There must be a reason.'

'Well there isn't. What's the reason for the tides, for the seasons? Yes, I know about the pull of the moon, the tilt of the earth and the heat of the sun. Those are causes, but are they a reason? Certainly not one you can fight, or argue with. Who do you want to be, King Canute standing on a beach with wet feet? Will you jump out of a plane without a parachute safe in the knowledge that you don't believe in gravity?'

'You're not helping,' said the Man.

'I think I am,' replied Hench.

Tooth slowly settled herself down on the stone of the hearth. After a moment, she allowed her heavy head to fall against her outstretched paw.

'I was going through my notes,' said the Man, gesturing towards the bureau. Make a note of that. Notes can be musical. Musical notes make a scale. A scale balances things and if it is the scale of justice then what it balances is right and wrong. Notes in the bureau are things that have been right as well as things have been written. These written rights aid us to remember. The notes in the inkwell are the most useful, ink being a medium of black and white.

'And what did you find?' said Hench.

'It's hard to say.'

'Hard to say because you don't know or hard to express exactly what you now know?'

'Fuck you, you clever cunt,' snaps the Man. 'I don't deserve this. I don't deserve it.'

Hench stood loose and limber. His arms hung by his sides like bullwhips ready to snap, like a scabbard that holds a sword. He is tender because he knows he has the capacity to be so cruel.

'No one does,' he said gently.

The Man sighed and levered himself out of his chair, walked softly across the kilims of embroidered memory to the window. 'Have you seen the trees?' he said.

Hench stood next to him. 'They're beautiful.'

'Yes, said the Man. 'But the colour, look at the colour.'

Hench looked at the Man. There had been a catch in his voice that he had never heard before. 'Autumn,' said the Man. 'In nearly sixty years there has never been an Autumn here, nor a Winter. Now look.'

For a little while they both stared at the rusting, gilded forest. It was a way to avoid looking at each other.

'How does it feel?' asked Hench at last.

'Like being robbed.' The Man sighed slowly. 'You go looking for something in yourself and it isn't there. A name. A face. A place. It's just gone. It's like being erased one piece at a time.'

'But to forget is...commonplace.'

The Man smashed his fist into the solid wood of the window shutter. 'To die is commonplace,' he spat.

Tooth looked up at the two men, her ears pricked; the hairs stood stiff along the line of her back and in her throat was the sound of a boulder rolling. Hench took the Man's hand and held it in the window light. The knuckles were skinned and there was a smear of blood.

'You were supposed to fight for me, said the Man. 'You were supposed to stand up for me, to go to war.'

'And yet, I cannot,' said Hench. 'I can't fight your greying hair as I can't fight the tide. I can't fight what brings the fear. All I can do is help you fight the fear itself.'

'It's not enough,' said the Man.

'It's all I have,' said Hench.

.

A tall candle, marked with the hours, burns down and the present dissolves into a pool of wax.

Hench stood on the Terrace of Sights and looked out towards the forest. The trees were black and leafless. The grasslands were browned, littered with thistle and teasel. There was flotsam and storm-tossed bladder wrack on the beach. The palace would not see another summer now.

At Hench's side stood Claw. The cold may have thickened her coat a little but it was hard to tell. She licked at Hench's hand. Even her tongue was strong and muscular. 'Come,' said Hench. 'Find him,' and Claw turned and led the way off the terrace.

As they walked through the palace Hench saw the signs of the damage done. One vaulted chamber was empty but for a chair on its side and a grand piano collapsed upon its legs. The ceiling had fallen and parts were strewn across the floor. It was impossible for Hench to guess what the Man might have remembered there.

Claw led him along one corridor after another. Some still appeared to be neat and tidy, solid and well maintained, but others showed signs of rot and decay. Tiles were missing from tessellated floors, wooden panelling bulged and bowed and wallpapered walls were water-stained and grievously marked.

In time, Claw padded through a low wooden door into the kitchen and there they found the Man standing with his back to them with Tooth at his side. Against one wall, a long beech work surface held two massive Belfast sinks and, above and behind it, a beech plate rack that must have held a hundred plates, each one different. The Man held one plate in his hands, eyes closed; he was breathing deeply relishing the aroma of a long-ago meal.

'Chez Gerrard. 1986. We had Chateaubriand, frites and two bottles of Brouilly. She was lovely. Name of Janet. We skipped desert for obvious reasons.' He let the plate fall to the floor where it shattered.

Hench and Claw stood silent. The Man took out the next plate.

'Bibendum. 1989. An incredible truffle mousse with a bottle of Muscadet and then Lapin à la Crème. It was the night we signed the contract with Harrison Lilly, but it's the meal that I remember.'

He let it fall to the flags.

'Grilled sardines on a beach in Crete. A salad dressed in olive oil and lemon.'

Another plate added to the shards.

'This is a pizza I cooked for my son. This one is a bacon sandwich on a rainy Saturday morning. Here is roast beef with everybody around the table. This is bread and cheese shared with Carol.'

The flagstone floor was carpeted in broken crockery. The Man's bare feet bled red roses across the white shrapnel of porcelain.

Hench had no words.

He wrapped his arms around the Man and cradled his head against his shoulder. Hench held him tight. Hench made him feel safe. It was all he could do.

.

In time the spring winds down, the pendulum ceases to rock and the hands no longer turn.

The palace lies in ruins, a memory of its former self.

Hench sometimes found the Man wandering the corridors and when he did he led him back to his chair by the fire in the Room of Living, which was where he mostly sat.

The Man too, was ruined.

His head was bald as an egg. His chin was stubbled and weak. The hard flesh had melted from his shoulders and arms and when he did walk it was with a slow shuffle in slippers that refused to stay on his feet. Mostly he sat in his chair with a blanket over his knees. Tooth or Claw always sat with him. Hench would put logs on the fire, tuck the blanket in from time to time, but they seldom spoke.

And one day, Hench decided that it was no longer safe.

The Room of Living had cracks in the ceiling and two of the walls. The fireplace looked unstable to Hench's eye. The day before, The Old Man had kicked out at Tooth as he lay by his side.

'It's time, I think,' said Hench. 'Time for the last thing I can do for you.'

The Old Man looked up at him. His eyes were rheumy. His lips were purple-black and glossy with spit. His skin was like crepe paper apart from across the bald dome of his skull where it was stretched tight as a drum skin. His ears and his nose; both seemed to have grown.

'Come with me,' said Hench and held out his hand. The Old Man shied away and cowered behind his bony shoulder and thin arm. Hench sank down on his haunches until he was lower than the Old Man. 'Come with me and I will take you somewhere safe,' he said in a voice as soft as warm milk.

Slowly, very slowly, Hench pulled the Old Man to his feet and, with Tooth and Claw walking at their side, they left the Room of Living for the last time. As they started down the long corridor, the Old Man slowly raised one hand till it rested on Hench's shoulder and gave him some support. They walked this way until their journey was done.

Hench stopped in front of a plain and simple wooden door. The door was nothing special, in fact it was a little smaller than most.

'In here,' Hench said. 'You will be safe. You must go in alone and you can never leave but you will be warm and safe, I promise you that.'

The Old Man looked at Hench and his eyes welled with tears, his breath became ragged and he licked wetly at his lips.

Just me?' he whispered and the tears began to flow. 'Is it just me now?'

Hench nodded. 'Well', he said at last. 'Look and then decide.'

Hench pushed the door open and stood back so that the Old Man could see inside. The room was a child's bedroom. There was a small bed with a colourful eiderdown thrown over the top. A big teddy bear was propped against the pillow and a little bear was by his side. There was a wooden box full of wooden toys and a knitted cat. Toy cars were lined up in a row on the threadbare carpet next to a toy castle that had obviously been made by the hand of a loving father.

'Oh, 'said The Old Man. 'I had forgotten this. I was happy here.'

'You can never come out again,' said Hench.

They stood in silence for a little time and then it seemed that the Old Man made up his mind. He looked at the bear and the toys and the cat. He looked at Hench and nodded. 'Yes please,' he said quietly and stepped through the open door. From somewhere far off in the palace came the sound of masonry falling to the ground.

The door to the nursery closed.

19:84

WINSTON LOOKED at the big clock on the wall. It was wrong.

'Your clock's wrong,' he said.

O'Brien twisted around in his chair and looked up at the wall behind him. Two or three feet above his head there was a big chunk of grey metal, a flat box with four rectangular windows in it. The windows were in pairs on either side of two cream dots. Each window showed two flat, grey plates, hinged in the middle with cream-coloured numbers printed on them. It was a mechanical, digital clock from the sixties. It was an ironic icon, a cute bit of kitsch.

The time it was showing was 19:84.

O'Brien frowned as he turned back to look at Winston across the slab of his beechwood desk. 'That's a bit judgemental,' he said. 'We try not to throw words like wrong around here. Wrong is a bit, well, wrong.'

'Yeah, it's still wrong though. You can't have nineteen eighty-four. Its...' Winston shrugged. 'It's too many numbers. Nineteen fifty-nine is the most it should be.'

O'Brien made a note on the pad in front of him. It didn't look like he'd drawn a smiley-face, it seemed more like a black mark to Winston. And to think, he'd thought O'Brien would be on his side.

'You need to be a bit more open-minded,' said O'Brien. 'The world's a big place. Lots of time zones and stuff like that. There's no reason to think that it can't be nineteen eighty-four somewhere out there is there?'

Winston winced. Perhaps this interview wasn't going to go as well as he'd hoped.

'Well let's car-park that for now. We can revisit it when we get to look at your PDS goals and deliverables,' said O'Brien and he smiled at Winston as if he had every confidence that the other man understood what had just been said.

'You've been working for us for, what, twelve years now, yes?'

'No.'

'Oh. Well, according to my records you've been working for TruthCorps since…'

'I've been here for the last two and a half years. Which is why I'm having my first annual performance review, I guess.'

O'Brien frowned. 'Well. We're here now so let's take a look at that performance, shall we?'

O'Brien looked to the large monitor screen on his desk. Winston could only see the back of it, the TruthCorps logo and a smudged sticker from IT showing a CE mark and when it had last been safety-tested. O'Brian twitched the mouse across his desk and his eyes flitted over the screen, left to right, top to bottom and back again. He pursed his lips and winced, he rolled the scroll wheel and sighed.

'Your numbers are down a bit recently. You seem less committed. Are you? Is that a fair assessment?'

Winston's eyebrows sank down his forehead like a pair of limp balloons. He swallowed and licked his lips. 'No. I don't think so,' he said a little too enthusiastically. 'I've always given a hundred and ten per cent and I still do.'

O'Brien raised a single eyebrow and his pen hovered over the pad once again.

'Hundred and twenty per cent,' said Winston quickly, shaking his head. 'Maybe more.'

'Good,' said O'Brien. 'That's good.'

Winston looked at the man who sat opposite him and wondered if he detested him at a personal level or if it was just because he was a type; like some sort of corporate version of racism. There certainly was plenty to detest. Conviction, dedication, seriousness and commitment surrounded O'Brien like a thick cloud of some malodorous body-spray. He probably doused himself with it every morning.

The way he supported his thoughtful chin in his capable hand, the way his eyes narrowed slightly with the intensity of his focus and the way he nodded his head in a movement that could only be measured in millimetres but let you know that he was urging you to think and say the right thing with every single solitary fibre of his being. His hair was immaculately cut. It looked like it was trimmed every single day. His stubble was a poem in facial hair. NASA couldn't work with any greater precision than this man's barber, thought Winston. There was a lot to hate.

And yet, there were two sides to this desk and he, Winston, was sitting on the wrong one.

'Good. It's just that some of your colleagues...' said

O'Brien. 'Some of your colleagues seem to think that you have lost faith, shall we say? They seem to think that you aren't totally on-board with where our business is going, moving forward, that is.'

Winston opened his mouth but O'Brien stopped him with a single raised finger.

'You see, here at TruthCorps, and I think you know this; everyone is a big cog in a big machine. That means I need you to believe completely in what we do and be passionate about what we do. That means we need you to be an evangelist for our brand and our product. So, do I hear a yes! Do I?'

'Who said I've lost faith?' said Winston.

'We can circle back on that,' said O'Brien. 'It's you that we're here to talk about.'

Winston folded his arms across his chest and turned away slightly in his chair.

'Look,' said O'Brien. 'I'm on your side. I get how you feel. I know where you're coming from. Things always seem to be changing around here and that can be difficult. Let's try this. At the core of things, what do you think TruthCorps is in the business of doing?'

'Reporting the news.'

O'Brien laughed. 'OK. I can see where the problem is. What do you think your job is?'

'Journalist.'

O'Brien sucked on his teeth. 'Right. Right.' He winced. 'You know your actual job title is Content Creator, right? Why do you think that is?'

'Oh, that's just because everything that goes on line is called content these days.'

'Well, OK. What about the "creator" part?'

'It's another word for writer.'

'Is it? Is it?'

O'Brien looked at the man who sat opposite him and wondered why on earth they were still employing dinosaurs like this. I mean, he thought, the guy must be in his forties! According to his records, he'd won a Pulitzer back in the day but what on earth did that mean in this day and age. Senior management probably thought his byline added a bit of credibility to some of the more outlandish stories but was that really worth the hassle?

O'Brien smiled at the man across the desk. His mouth moved to make the right shape but his eyes didn't get the memo. Still, who cares? Winston was smiling back at him.

O'Brien suddenly realised that Winston's stubble was the result of poor shaving, not exquisite grooming. He could even see nasal hair. My god, the man was practically an ape! How was he going to move the needle on this relic? He oozed cynicism. Sure, he was trying to hide it, but O'Brien could tell. His jacket actually was crumpled, it wasn't tailored to look that way. There was something that looked suspiciously like a pen, maybe even a biro, in his shirt pocket. It was hard to believe but the problem was, and O'Brien let his attention return to his monitor, if you looked at his stats the guy was good. Hell, a few years ago, he'd been great. His click-through rates were impressive and if you used the longer attribution model they were even more so. The dude could write. His likes and shares had been up there with the best of them but there was a definite falling off. The guy's heart just wasn't in it anymore. And the thing was, his line manager had tried. They had him working in the alt-right section and then moved him over to concerned-liberal. The last six months he'd been in eco-worried but even all that "save the planet" shit didn't seem to gel with him. It was almost as if he didn't want to put a spin on the stories. Christ, where would we be if everyone thought like that?

O'Brien templed his fingers and touched their tips to his lips. Let's try and get him back on board, he thought, but I'm not going to boil the ocean on this one.

'Do you know what we sell here, at TruthCorps?'

'The news? Online syndicated news stories?'

'No,' said O'Brien. 'We sell attention. We generate content that is perhaps news related but definitely attention-grabbing and then our clients buy that attention from us so they can show people their message. That's what we do. We sell attention.'

'That's not how I see it.'

'Then you're wrong. What do you think? Do you think you'd rather be back in the golden age of journalism? Some Fleet Street wino ceaselessly dedicated to finding the truth and investigating the issues of the day. That isn't how it was. That was never how it was.'

Winston folded his arms higher up on his chest and leant back further in his chair. Beneath the desk, he started jiggling his foot.

'Those newspapers that you wish you were still writing for were in the same business as us. They put something that grabbed the consumer's attention on the front page and then filled the rest of the thing with advertising space that they sold to their clients. They were selling attention.'

Winston looked down at the perfect surface of the beechwood desk. There was a fly crawling across it in that alien, jerky stuttering way that they do. He wanted to squash it but he knew it was much too fast for him.

'That might be how the business model works but the news is still the news. We shouldn't change it or make it up or write it from a different perspective or...'

'Oh, come on.' O'Brien leaned forward. 'Put the same story in a left-wing broadsheet and a right-wing tabloid. Is it going to look the same, read the same?'

'Well, no.'

'Well, no. Exactly.' O'Brien shook his head dismissively. 'We do what's always been done. We just do it better. What do you think news is, anyway?'

For a second, Winston was flustered. 'Well its, umm? News is current affairs, world events.'

O'Brien shook his head.

'It's information about recent events. It's newly received stuff.'

'It's entertainment.'

Winston lurched forward. 'I won't have that,' he said. The news is important. It's how people get to know what's happening in the world and how they inform their opinions and how society stays...'

'Oh crap,' said O'Brien and rocked back in his executive leather and chrome chair. He looked at the wall to the left of him. It was made of frosted glass and the silhouettes of other staff walked to and fro across it like tracing paper cut-outs in a shadow play. You could almost see the strings that moved them, the puppeteer's sticks that made them dance and jig,

'If you want to know what is going on in the world, there is data and there are statistics and there are facts. People can find these things. They are on the Internet. Like we are. But they don't. They click on your miserable stories about how pets are contributing to climate change and how disposable contact lenses are polluting the oceans and killing dolphins. They click on your headlines about how carbon emissions from back-yard barbecues are melting the ice caps and which twenty-five animals scientists want to bring back from extinction. I am right, aren't I? Those are all your stories?'

'That was the content that my department head briefed me to…'

'Oh. You're getting it now, are you? Did any of those stories inform people? Did they help them to make better decisions? No. They gave them a little thrill of, Ooh everything is so awful, and then they let them go on with their day while blithely ignoring the bigger picture.'

Winston tried to hold O'Brien's gaze but he failed. His eyes dropped to the desk top and then to his hands. He was rubbing his hands together. He slid them beneath the table. He was tempted to sit on his fingers to make sure that he couldn't wring his hands but that was just going to look worse. This was turning into his worst nightmare. It really was.

O'Brien pushed the pad away and set his pen down. 'Look,' he said. 'I think we should get all this out in the open but I've got a conference call in two minutes, I need to loop back to another team on something, then I can look under the bonnet with you again. I don't want you on my radar. I want you on board or I'm going to sunset you, alright?'

Utterly confused, Winston nodded.

O'Brien made little 'get up' motions with his hands. 'So can you give me the room for five?' he said.

As Winston was walking towards the door he turned and looked back at the other man. 'They weren't really miserable were they?' he said. 'My stories, I thought that…'

O'Brien shook his head, held up an open palm and said, 'Five. OK.'

Closing the office door behind him, Winston emerged onto a balcony that ran all the way around an absolutely enormous space. He saw the place every single working day and yet it never ceased to shock him: tens of thousands of square metres under one roof. It was the open-plan office to end all open-plan offices. Looking down on it from the balcony, the floor below looked like a landscape. There were yellow-themed breakout areas that resembled beaches by the sea. Coffee stations and food stops that looked like glades and patches of woodland. There was so much IT down there that there were actually server hubs on the floor, totem poles of smoked glass and aluminium with lights flashing away inside to show that the data gods were still alive. Most of all there were workstations, the cubicles. Winston had heard someone saying that over two and half thousand people worked in this space and most of them were trapped in two-metre-square pens that had just enough room for a desk, a monitor, a chair and a person. They were the human batteries that ran this matrix, the softest of the software.

From the balcony, Winston was an explorer looking down on a foreign land from the safety of a balloon floating amongst the clouds and the clouds were the shining silver tubes of air-handling pipework and the convoluted knots of ducted cooling systems. Above the hum of the air conditioning fans, a low, droning noise filtered up from the floor below, the sound of worker bees, the sound of mumbled prayer, the sound of the future.

The balcony ran straight and true for what appeared

to be hundreds of meters in each direction. On one side a smoked glass panel and a wooden handrail, on the other numbered office doors and frosted glass walls. This was a management suite and "opaque" seemed to be the keyword for the decoration.

One of the office doors opened and O'Brien stepped out onto the balcony. He came and stood next to Winston, both of them with their hands on the rail and leaning out over the void.

'Big cogs in a big machine?' said Winston.

'Perhaps it's a matter of perspective,' said O'Brien looking at the teeming midgets below. 'Or perception, or some such.'

Winston sighed. 'Watching them, watching others, watching us. I hate the whole Big Brother thing.'

O'Brien shrugged, nonplussed.

'You know, Big Brother is always watching you. It's from that book.'

'Dunno,' said O'Brien. 'If you're talking about the data that we keep I'm absolutely not going to guilt-trip on that.'

'Well data is a nice little, neutral word for it don't you think? It's a bit more than data, surely. It's what they believe, what they think, what they feel, what they do.'

'And it's not as if we steal it from them, is it? Just give 'em a smart phone and a couple of networking platforms and you simply can't shut the buggers up. From what they had for dinner to their…'

'Sexual orientation.'

'Oh, purleeese. Don't go there. Our servers have got nudes of half the bloody people in the western hemisphere so I'm not listening to a thing about invasions of privacy, OK?'

Winston explored the inside of his mouth with his tongue, trying to find a grain of truth. 'I suppose they are a bit naïve,' he eventually said. 'Everything we said we'd do was written there if they could be bothered to look.'

'Exactly.'

Winston nodded. 'One thing though, you've got my data wrong. You said I'd been working here for twelve years. I haven't. It's only been a couple of years.'

O'Brien smirked. 'You started at NewsDaily, yeah? We own that. Then you were at TruthSearcher. We own that through a holding company. Then you went to...?' He looked at Winston, furrowing his brow.

'I had a year at FriendFinder, before they went bust.'

'Odd choice. They didn't go bust by the way. We bought them out and shut them down. Easiest way of staying on top. Then…'

'Yeah, OK. I get it.'

'Well, you know. It is what it is. Come back in here for a minute. There's something I think will make you see things our way.'

O'Brien held the office door open and ushered Winston inside. On the door was the room number, one-oh-one, and a little sliding sign that O'Brien flicked over from vacant to occupied.

They sat down again, Winston on the wrong side of the desk and O'Brien on the other. The wall clock still said 19:84. O'Brien started to tap away at his keyboard, taking occasional glances at the screen.

'Rats,' he said.

'What?' said Winston, alarmed.

'Oh nothing. I want to show you something but I've forgotten my password.' O'Brien frowned. 'I wonder if it was… Ah, good. We're in. I just need you to put something on a minute.' He reached into a desk drawer and produced a VR headset that he pushed across the table to Winston. It was a box that sat over his face with straps and buckles to hold it in place.

Winston put it on. As soon as he did so he started to do the weird head movements that people do when exploring a virtual space. 'What am I looking at?' he said.

'That my friend is a disruptive game changer within the content solutions industry. That is the future. Well, it's an interface to the future.'

'It looks like a video game.'

'In a way, it is. Gamifying something often makes the people who are using it more productive. It gets them to work faster and for longer,'

'Nice.'

'Tell me what you see.'

Winston's head did some big rolling gestures. Up and down, left and right. 'I'm in a building,' he said. 'It's like a labyrinth. Like an Escher painting but like a real building as well. Is it some sort of library? It's huge. Bigger than the work floor out there. It's…massive.'

'The space here, that space we were just looking at a couple of minutes ago, is as big as we know how to build but it's already too small so we've built this. This place is infinite. We'll never outgrow it. We simply can't.'

'And, err…what's it for?'

'The real and the virtual both do the same thing. Stories, subjects, things to create content about, come in and they are given to a particular content guy…'

'Writer.'

'Whatever. Writer then. A particular guy or guys to

write up in a way that will appeal to a specific audience.'

'Like the alt-right or the eco-worried?'

'Yep.'

'So what I'm looking at is a virtual newsroom? A fake newsroom?'

'Yep.'

'But I still don't understand why we need this.'

'It's the only way to handle the capacity and the speed.'

'Speed?' said Winston. 'It takes anyone an hour or so to write a thousand-word piece, say. So why do we need speed? There's no point in working at any pace faster than a writer can write.'

'We've solved that too. Let me run the demo and you'll see. I'd hang on to your lunch though.' O'Brien tapped at his keyboard and then hit enter. Winston jerked back as if a brick had hit him. 'My god,' he grunted.

'Fast, huh.'

'But the stories must all be queuing up. It's doing the allocation but not the writing.'

'Look to the right, where the docs are going in to delivery tubes.'

'It's finished content. How is that even happening?'

'AI,' said O'Brien. 'Machines are writing it. Fast little mothers, aren't they?'

And Winston screamed.

And screamed.

And screamed.

Two hours later, Charrington was sitting on the edge of O'Brien's desk swinging his Gucci loafers to and fro.

'He's back at work then,' said Charrington.

'Yeah. For now.'

'That's good. I don't like to see too much churn in the

department. It raises eyebrows upstairs in the c-suite. Do you think he'll last?'

'I do actually,' said O'Brien.

'You frightened him that much? The thought that he could be replaced by a machine?'

'Oh no. That's not what did it. I went old-school. I told him that he was a special case, a special talent and that I could see his point of view and that he could write his stories, generate his content as he saw fit. That he should tell the truth without spin.'

Charrington's foot stopped mid-swing and his manicured fingers gripped the edge of the desk. He glowered at O'Brien.

'Don't lose your shit,' said O'Brien. 'I lied. He reckons he's a journo, right? Proper honest to goodness, old school reporter?'

Charrington nodded.

'So I told him to write the truth. His truth. Describe the world as he sees it, in complete honesty,' and O'Brien smiled. 'Then we just distribute his content to the woolly-minded-liberals and the chattering-classes. They'll lap it up. They'll be so busy writing politically correct comments and firing off concerned emojis that they'll never lift a finger against us.'

'Very neat,' said Charrington. 'Very neat indeed.'

He looked up at the wall above O'Brien's head. 'You do know your clock's wrong, don't you?'

O'Brien rolled his eyes. 'Honestly, you people think irony is like "silvery" and "goldy", don't you? Has no one around here got a fucking sense of humour?'

NAMES IN THE SAND

'HOW ARE you feeling?'

'I'm OK.'

'No really, how are you feeling?'

The old man in the chair thought for a moment or two. He looked at the oxygen cylinder by his side and the blanket over his knees. He looked at his hand that was skeletal and tattooed with ink-dark bruises and blue-black veins. 'Sometimes there's pain,' he said. 'But it's not too bad. Not too bad at all, thank you.'

Pete looked at his father. He tilted his head gently to one side and bit his lip. Seemingly of their own volition, his thumbs rubbed against his fingertips, nervous and uncertain.

'Are you sure?' he asked. 'The doctors have said that there's no reason for you to be in pain. That they can take it away.'

'Well,' said the old man in the chair. 'There's time enough for that, isn't there? I'm all right. Honestly, I'm all right.'

Pete shrugged. 'I'm going into town. Can I get you

anything?'

'Are you going to the garage?'

'What do you want? If you tell me what you want, I'll get it.'

'If you're going to the garage then I could do with some milk,' said the man in the chair. 'Pick me up a small milk.'

'Pump number three and this,' said Pete to the man in the garage passing him a litre carton of milk.

'That comes to twenty-one pounds ninety. Would you like a receipt to give to the VAT man?

Pete shook his head. 'It's starting to get quieter, isn't it?'

'That it is, young man, and not before time. Much as I dearly love all our visitors I am never as happy as when I see the fuckers leave.'

'Schools go back…when? Next week, isn't it?'

'That it is, young sir. And then we have the beach to ourselves again. I can go for a walk without the obstruction of piles of bodies.'

'Oh, come on. You'll miss 'em.'

'To be honest, no I won't. I really won't.' John smiled and handed Pete's card back to him.

After walking back to the car, Pete dropped the milk on the passenger seat, buckled up and turned the key. He pulled the big old Merc away from the pump and up to the road. Turn left meant go back home, turn right for a drive through town.

Well, there was nothing to do at home, nothing at all, so five minutes later Pete pulled in at the end of Beach Road.

The end of the Summer was getting closer but it hadn't arrived yet.

In the Winter, the beach was a painting. A smudged landscape, sea-grey and sky-blue, where charcoal stick figures throw balls for dogs and out in the sea rubber-black surfers climb foaming, treacherous peaks.

But in the Summer, it's a postcard. A saucy, salacious snapshot of too much flesh exposed to too much sun. Kiss me quick but hold me tight. Wish you were here, lots of love from Aunty Dot and your cousin Vi.

In the Summer you can stand on the promenade next to the car park and look out over three-and-a-bit miles of beach and be forgiven for thinking that you can't see a single grain of sand. People? Yes. You can see fat people, thin people, young people and old; the flotsam and jetsam of fifty working weeks somewhere up north. Up where the tributaries of the M5 and M6 begin to run down towards the sea. All of them are here it seems, on this beach.

At low tide they thin out and trickle down towards the surf line, some even get grabbed by the breakers and bob about in the shallows, but when the tide starts to come back in it pushes them up the beach like spume and they become stuck in drifts around the ice cream stand and the place where Bob's kids sell cold Cokes from rusty oil drums filled with ice.

And every one of those thousands of people leaves their own mark.

No one steps onto the sand without leaving an impression, without leaving a record of his or her passage. Writing not their name in the sand, although enough of them do that, but the trail of their journey. Perhaps they built a castle. Perhaps they marked out a volleyball court.

Perhaps they used the sand as a canvas and drew a face or, they simply looked back at their own footprints and marvelled that the print left behind was unique to them.

And twice a day that record is wiped away; all trace removed.

Twice a day the tide comes in and drives them back to the dunes, back to the rocks and, at high tide itself, off the beach entirely. Later, when time has passed and the tide has turned the beach emerges from the sea once again and shows no trace of what had been at all.

No mark. No record. Nothing.

Pete looked out at the beach and wondered what it was that so fascinated him about it. It's a picture post-card full of life where his own life is slowly getting filled with death, albeit not his own.

That could be it.

He slips the Merc into Drive and turns for home.

.

A month or so later Summer's end had arrived.

The sky was seldom blue. Any warmth that could be found was in the colour of the leaves still clinging to the trees, their rich yellows and golden hues like a sketchbook page from the Summer gone. There was more rain, more wind. The tourists had long drained away and the town began to show a leaner face, a fossil emerging from the wind-blown sand.

'How are you feeling?'

'I'm not too bad.'

'No really, how are you feeling?'

The old man in the chair is thinner now. His bones

protrude through his skin, even through his clothes. His skull is clearer to see. There is less of him. Interesting things happen at the borders, thinks Pete, as he looks at his father who is a man approaching the border between life and death.

'What did we used to say? As well as can be expected. That was it, wasn't it?' Crepe paper skin crinkled around the old man's eyes. 'Are you going into town?'

'Yes,' says Pete, even though he wasn't.

'Get me a What's On will you? You know the thing? They keep it on the magazine rack near the bottom. On the left-hand side usually. If you can't find it, ask the lady.'

The door shuts behind Pete and when the old man knows he is alone he breaks down into the coughing fit that he has been hiding for the last few minutes. He looks at the tiny splash of blood on the back of his hand.

'Fuck,' he says to himself and his god.

.

Out of season the Co-Op car park has plenty of spaces, more than enough for everyone. In the Autumn, the population has been culled from its summertime peak. In the Autumn, it's faces that are lacking, not space.

'Haven't seen you for a while,' said the woman behind the till.

'I try and avoid you in the Summer,' says Pete, smiling. 'You and the fifteen thousand other happy campers just waiting to brighten my day.' He dumps his basket of shopping next to the till.

'Do you want a bag?" she asks. 'A five-pee bag or a bag-for-life?'

'Five-pee's fine. There's something slightly odd about having a bag that promises to outlive you.'

The woman puts a flimsy plastic bag on the counter and starts to ring up Pete's shopping.

'Good Summer, did you?' he asks.

'You can't imagine,' she laughs. 'It's as if they've never been in a supermarket before. It's as if coming in here was part of their holiday experience. They literally stand and stare at the shelves like they were from another planet. And the rush at five o'clock! They come off that beach like I don't know what. My Lord, they do.'

Pete grumbled some sound of agreement. 'How's himself?' he asks.

She looks up at him. 'My dear husband? He's as bad if not worse. The day he dies, I'm leaving all this.' She looks around at the shop. 'The very day.' She blinks hard, two or three times. 'The memory thing, losing his memory, that I can live with but the anger?' She shakes her head. 'I can't tell you about the anger.'

Pete swallows hard and he almost reaches out to take her hand, but no. All of his shopping has gone from basket to bag. All except the copy of What's On magazine which the woman holds out to him. While she was talking she rolled it and rolled it until it's wrapped tight as a stick. He gently takes the magazine from her hands, nods at the jam-packed carrier bag then lifts the rolled magazine up with a shrug. 'What am I supposed to do with this?' he asks. She looks him dead flat in the eye and says 'You can stick it up your arse for all I care.'

Pete gives her a little smile. 'I'll see you around, then,' he says. 'You take care now,' and carrying the bag in one hand and What's On in the other he leaves the shop.

.

Pete parks the Merc in the beachfront car park and stares out to sea. At least, he assumes the sea is there.

The coast is that never-ending line where sea and land meet. It's a border state, a margin. A beach is that and more. It's constantly impermanent. Becoming more one thing and then the other as time and tide shift. A beach is sea you can walk on, land that drowns. The beach in front of Pete seems even less solid than that. Sea, sky and sand blur together into a vapour. The beach is big, very big and very flat. The tide, if it is out there, is out a long way, far too far for Pete to see. Perhaps there is a line where the haze is slightly whiter, where it boils into the sky. That might be the surf line. It might not. Spray is lifted from the waves and spreads across the landscape painting it in layers and layers of shapes and shades of blueish-grey. The sky reflected on marooned water sitting mirror-flat on the sand.

All the elements are out of place, time seems out of joint.

Pete feels as if he should be able to poke a finger-hole in the diaphanous view and see through into another place but when he gets out of the car a deep chill tells him not to go exploring, not to walk the beach today. A cold hand pressing against his cheek, pushing him away.

'Not stretching your legs then?'

Pete turns and sees John standing behind him.

'Scare someone to death you will,' says Pete. 'Creeping up behind them and all.'

'I prefer to think of it as treading lightly on the earth.'

'Oh, right. I don't know how well that sits with selling

petrol for thirty bloody years. You little one-man oil slick, you.'

John laughs. 'Well, it's nice to be appreciated, young man.' He stands with his weight thrown on one leg. His arms hang limply at his sides and his long, scrawny neck supports a thin, hollow-cheeked face tanned to the shade of old shoe leather.

'Funny how much it changes, isn't it?'

'The beach?'

'Yeah,' says John. 'Six weeks past you couldn't see it for people and now there's not a living soul out there.'

'And you can still hardly see the bloody thing,' says Pete peering at the misty blur. 'You not working today?'

'No. Not today, young man. Definitely not today.' John pulls a pack of cigarettes from his pocket and lights one.

'They'll be the death of you,' says Pete. John almost smiles as he takes a long pull. 'I doubt it,' he replies. 'I really doubt it.'

The two men stand in silence for a little while looking out at the blank beach.

'I retire next month,' says John. 'Well, I call it being fired but they are using the retired word. I don't understand why. I think they'll get some teenager to do my job for half the money. Will you miss me?'

Pete wrinkles his brow. Raises his open hands.

'Yeah,' says John, rather quietly. 'I know. Well, 'bye then. Enjoy the view.' He walks past Pete, on to the beach and out onto the sand leaving his footprints trailing behind him. After a minute the mist closes in over his shape and the trail of his prints lead out across the sand to absolutely nothing at all.

Pete waits for a little while, just standing by the car. He

watches the blank mist to see if John will reappear. There had been something about him, a sadness that made Pete feel guilty that they hadn't talked longer, that he hadn't said that, yes, of course he'd miss him.

Reluctantly, Pete steps out on to the sand and follows John's tracks, the soles of his trainers leaving a distinctive pattern, regular and deeply incised. The rest of the sand, as far as Pete can see in the mist, is as smooth and untouched as fresh plaster. As he walks the mist wraps itself around him, a damp grey blanket that deadens his senses. After a time, he looks over his shoulder but can barely see the car park. When he looks down, even John's footprints have faded to merely the faintest outline.

Then there is nothing.

Pete stands in a soft grey world that has no features at all. The mist is so uniform that even up and down seem irrelevant terms. He wants to shout John's name; at the same time he's scared to make any noise at all. A seagull flies above him in total silence, a ghost spirit.

He turns around and around until he sees a single line of footprints that can only be his own, a skein leading back through a labyrinth, a lifeline, an umbilicus.

.

'How are you feeling?'

'Not too bad.'

'Really?'

The old man is standing by his chair, one hand on its arm. Barely moving. Barely breathing.

'Thank you for taking me.'

'It's nothing. Not a problem. The least I can…um.'

'We shouldn't be long, should we?'

'No. We shouldn't be long. Why?'

'It's nothing. I'll be fine. It's just that…I'm not dying there. You know. I don't want to end like that.'

Pete pushes his hands deep into his trouser pockets. His fingers want to writhe in anguish. At least the pockets hide them. He can pretend to be calm.

'I don't want to die in hospital,' says his father. 'I don't want to be on a bed… behind a curtain… when they close it for the last time. I don't want that.' His lip trembles even though he hasn't shown a truly honest emotion for years.

'Please,' Pete says, and a wave of desolation drenches his body. His hands lie still. Nodding his head towards the door he says, 'Come on. We need to go.'

'Do you promise?' asks his father. 'Will you promise me?'

.

By late November, the town is truly a ghost of its Summer self. The wind has left sand dunes on the pavements. Half the shops have put up rusty shutters or fast-fading notes that appear in empty, white-washed windows saying, "Closed till June. Leave post next door." Summer-coloured signs still incongruously offer ice cream, slush puppies and beach goods but even the dogs that are dragged past squint into the sandblast gale that whips in from the sea.

Pete, sitting in the parked-up Merc, can hear the white noise of the breakers roaring at the water's edge but he can't see them. The wind is a thunderous turbine-roar firing spume and drizzle against the windscreen so hard that it rocks the car. The engine is running so that the de-mister works and the inside of the car is warm and snug. Next to him on the passenger seat is a copy of the local paper and he glances down from time to time at the picture on the front page.

Pete drives down to the seafront to look at the beach, not perhaps every day, but he seldom misses two days in a row. He's starting to know it now, its moods and its tempers. The beach has been here forever, a beast breathing in and out with each successive tide. Sometimes that beast is angry, sometimes playful. Sometimes the beach lies sleeping and sometimes, on those topsy-turvy, misty and mercurial days, the beach dreams.

Pete is beginning to get worried about the beach.

He takes another glance at the picture of John above the headline, Popular Local Man Still Missing. He puts the car into gear and drives back to the garage, the one where John used to work.

'Pump number six, please. Oh, has What's On come in yet or am I too soon?'

'They are over there, bottom of the rack,' says the woman who owns the garage. She yawns behind her hand.

'What about John then, eh?' asks Pete, handing her the magazine.

'You never really know people do you?' she replies.

'What do you mean?'

'He always seemed happy enough with that bloody silly sense of humour of his, but then…' She hands Pete the card machine.

'Then what?'

'Turns out his wife left him last year and he'd never said a thing. The only reason they discovered he was missing was because Norma, she lives next door, works at the Co

Op. Know who I mean? Well, Norma saw he hadn't put his recycling out.'

'Norma with the husband with Alzheimer's?'

'Dementia.'

'Whatever.'

The door opens and a little family spill in out of the cold. The kids grab bags of sweets and the adults start pressing buttons on the cappuccino machine.

'Would you have fired him if you'd known? You know, if you knew he was on his own would you still have fired him?'

The garage lady gives him a look straight from Siberia.

'VAT receipt?' she asks.

Pete shakes his head.

.

Pete knocks on the kitchen door and after a minute the net curtain is twitched back and an eye peers out at him. He smiles. The curtain falls back into place and Pete can hear the sound of one…two…three locks being turned before the door opens.

'They're not for the burglars,' she says. 'I'm not worried about burglars. It's him. He'd be out and off down the road like a shot. Not that I know why that's such a bad idea, I really don't. Come in, as you're here.'

Pete steps into the kitchen.

'Who is it?' says a man's voice from somewhere in the house. 'Who is it? Tell them to sod off. Tell them we don't want any.'

Norma shakes her head and shrugs. 'See what I mean?' she says. 'Who'd put up with that all day, every day?'

'Just tell them to sod off, you stupid cow,' shouts her husband and Norma softly shuts the kitchen door.

Pete stands by the sink. His head leans to one side, then the other. He scratches his chin and chews his lip. He takes a deep breath in but…

'Oh just spit it out,' says Norma. 'You've come about John.'

'I saw him. On the beach,' says Pete.

'Sit down,' she says and pulls a chair from under the kitchen table. 'He came and said goodbye. You know, before he…' Norma studies her fingernails, perfectly painted a hideous pale blue. She looks up. 'I wouldn't have noticed his recycling wasn't out in a month of Sundays. I've got my own problems,' and she nods towards the voice grumbling away in the back of the house.

Norma took a big breath in then, with a sigh, she lets the story out. 'No wife, no job, no point. I think that's how he saw it. You or I might have taken a pill but for John, it was the beach. It was always going to be the beach. John was born here, you see,' says Norma. 'Not an incomer. His family had been here for generations. Stories get passed down. He knew about the beach.'

'What did he know?'

'He wasn't scared. He didn't think it would hurt. He said his Nan had told him that it was probably like falling asleep. You'd just fade away like a sea fret. Of course, she was telling him stuff to stop him going out there. You know, like don't play on the railway tracks and don't go near the edge.'

'So what is it?' said Pete, frowning. 'What is it?'

Norma laughed. 'Do you think I know that? And I've thought about it some, I can tell you. I've a mind to an idea but whether it's true?' and she shook her head, her lacquered, grey curls bouncing stiffly.

'Go on,' says Pete.

'Perhaps there are places where the world gets thin,' she says. 'You don't so much fall off as fall through. I don't know. Sometimes people go missing. Sometimes people who walk on the beach go missing. You've been watching it, haven't you? That beach. I've heard you've been watching it.'

Norma stands and goes to the sink to fill the kettle. 'Do you want a coffee?' she says. 'I don't get many visitors.' Pete can hear swearing from the other room but he says yes anyway.

'But why?' Pete asks.

'Why?' says Norma. 'He just didn't have anything left. At least, that's how he saw it. No more Betty at home, and no more reason to go out. That job, it was all the social life he had left. Same as for me, really. They could have kept him on at the garage. They could have done that for him.'

'I don't think they knew,' says Pete. 'I don't think they even knew that Betty had gone.'

Norma's face freezes in sadness as the kettle boils and steams up the kitchen window. A single droplet of condensation runs slowly down through the blurred view.

·

'I'm sorry,' says the old man in the chair. 'But it sounds like nonsense, to me.'

'But he just disappeared. He vanished. I saw him.'

'Well that's rather the point,' said the old man. 'You didn't see him. Look, Pete, I know this hasn't been easy for you. I know you can be rather delicate, just like your Mother.'

'Oh for fucks…'

'Don't get upset now. I know you care and that you're worried about what will happen but this? This is just nonsense. It's an old wives' tale.'

'Norma told me that…'

'And Norma's not having the best of times either, is she? Maybe you just lost his trail? Maybe it got washed away? Maybe he sank up to his neck in quicksand? I don't know. But did the beach eat him? I don't think so.'

Pete sits down at the table and begins to fiddle with one of the coasters. He rolls it through his fingers like a cardsharp waiting for the game. He looks at his father. 'You don't want to die in hospital,' he says.

'And you don't want to look after me here,' replies the old man.

'That's not fair,' says Pete.

'I don't think much in life is, do you?'

Pete slams the coaster down on the table. 'What if it's true? What if I just drive you down to the beach and you walk out on to the sand and somehow slip away and…'

'Go to a better place?' sneers his father. Then he begins to cough. It starts as a heaving in his chest where it seems to be trapped for a while. Pete gets up and leans over his father but the old man turns away, retching and gasping and hawking onto the back of his hand where both men see a small red clot amongst the phlegm.

'How long?' asks Pete.

'The blood?' he says. 'It's been a few weeks now. Quite a few weeks.'

'You didn't say.'

The old man shrugs. The two men look at each other and all around them the thunderous stream of time turns their past into their future. Pete reaches out to his father for the first time in many, many years and they hold each other's hand.

'They won't let me stay here, will they?'

'All the way to the end?' whispers Pete. 'Probably not.'

'So it'll be the hospital, on plastic sheets and behind a nylon curtain. With drips and tubes and strangers poking me and no chance for a pipe of baccy.'

Pete squeezes his father's hand.

'Those my choices, are they?' says the old man. 'A fairy tale or a horror story? Some way to end, isn't it?'

.

The Merc bounces over the speed bumps on Beach Road. It's only just after eight o'clock but at this time of year the town hardly wakes up at all before midday. The streets are deserted, the shops are still closed and the car park is empty but for two small figures standing next to a Nissan Micra.

Pete rolls the Merc to a stop. He can recognise Norma from here.

Beyond the car park, the beach has dissolved into a miasma of air, sea and sand. A fine mist blows inshore and sand swirls around at ankle level.

The world is thin here. Time and tide have worn it away. Dreams and desperation are a little too close to the surface.

Pete puts his hand on the car door handle. He swings it open.

'Leave me alone, you cow. I don't want to go for a walk. Not with you. Who are you? I don't know you.' The man's voice is hollow, as empty as the mist.

Norma leads him closer and closer towards the beach. 'Come on, Rodger,' she says. 'Just a short walk. It'll do you good.'

Pete leaves the car and steps towards them. Rodger winces and avoids Norma's hand as it reaches for his. He peers suspiciously at the world, his eyebrows plunge into a deep, angry frown but his eyes are pale and scared. Only his voice is brave. 'Off me! Get off me.'

Pete is closer now.

'Rodger, come on,' she snaps. 'We need to do this. I need you to do this.'

'Who are you?' he wails. She snatches his hand out of the air and tugs him so hard that he stumbles. Pete jerks forwards as if to catch him.

'I don't want to,' he says. 'I don't want to. I don't know you.' He hugs his arms in around his thin chest. 'Where's Norma. If Norma were here she would give you what for. Norma would look after me. My Norma.'

Norma steps back as if slapped. Her jaw hangs slack. She almost forgets to breathe.

'My Norma would look after me,' says Rodger through the tears that wash his face in the fine mist.

'This isn't right,' says Pete. 'It isn't right.'

Norma looks at him. 'Who are you to say? Who are you to say what's right?'

'He doesn't know, Norma. He doesn't know what you are trying to do. How is that right?'

Norma looks at him in bitter anger. 'And how much time will I have left? How much life will I have left after…' She sighs. 'Prick,' she spits at him then gently leads her husband back towards the car.

'Perhaps Norma's at home,' Pete hears her say. 'Let's go and see,' and he watches their car disappear out of the car park.

He looks around. Pale grey mist. Pale grey sky. He hears the beach exhale and the cold air chills his skin. The breakers tumble over each other somewhere out of sight. It's always been like this. Sea you can walk on, land that drowns, time that slips.

Pete opens the passenger door of the car and leans inside. 'Come on, Dad,' he says. 'Come on. I think I might come with you.'

IF A TREE FALLS

AILEEN, BRIAN, Caroline, Dylan and Eleanor. Those are the storms that we've had over the Winter and it's only what, mid-February?

It's Eleanor that brings about the end of our world. Or saves it, or starts it up again, depending on your point of view. Well, Eleanor and me, obviously. I can't excuse myself from the responsibility for what I expect is going to happen but I thought that, should anyone survive, it was only right that I leave some sort of record of what I did and why. And the thing is, I don't know if I'm asking for your thanks or your forgiveness.

So, where does it all begin? With the storms, I guess.

For lots of people it was all a bit of a joke wasn't it? We'd been talking about global warming and greenhouse gases for years and years and all that seemed to be happening was that each and every year it got colder and wetter. And that let people off the hook. Sure, we all thought that we should do our bit and show the right level of concern when it came to carbon emissions, coal-fired power stations and those dodgy Germans who cheated on the facts about their diesel engines but 'cold and wet' doesn't play very well when it comes to scaring people, does it? 'Cold and wet' doesn't look like a precipice that you are about to fall off. A shot of a skinny polar bear doesn't rack up against footage of a good old African famine. The ice caps may well be melting but there still seems to be rather a lot of them and anyway, who actually goes there? What are ice caps even for? So we all paid lip service to reducing our carbon footprint and we all talked about 'stepping lightly on the earth' but at the end of the day, ninety-nine per cent of people did absolutely fuck-all about it. Me included, you understand. I'm no saint in this. I'm just as likely to be remembered as the devil, if there's anyone left to remember me at all that is.

But really, what were we all thinking?

Putting the recycling out on Sunday evening and trying to use the car a bit less. Is that the behaviour you would expect from someone faced with, not their own death perhaps, but the imminent death of their children or their children's children? Is it? We spent hundreds of years obsessing about what future generations would think of us and then, all of a sudden, when there might not be any more future generations, it was all just that bit too much to cope with. We decided that a big new car every few years or one of those machines that make you an espresso out of little aluminium bullet or not having any wind turbines spoiling the view from the house, that was all far more important.

But we were all concerned. Of course, we were all concerned as fuck. And the best way to let everyone know that was to say the right thing. Pay lip service and say the right words, Parrot the right phrases.

'We all need to be environmentally friendly,' and 'I'm just so eco-conscious these days.' What about, 'Be an eco-warrior and defend the planet.' I mean, what the actual fuck?

I used to think, 'Save the planet' was a particularly badly chosen one. The planet was going to be fine, it was the people who were fucked. The planet didn't give a shit. The planet didn't care.

Turns out I may not have been entirely right about that.

.

Aileen, Brian, Caroline, Dylan and Eleanor. They might have all had different names but it seemed as if you could hardly slip a fag paper between them. As soon as one blew over another was there to take its place.

For months I had been going to bed with the sound of the wind tearing at the farmhouse roof and the rain rattling on the windows. Waking in the night to a roaring gale. Getting up in the morning to low, grey skies and sheets of drizzle flapping across the fields. The occasional sunny, dry day was like finding a single Quality Street in your pocket; a lovely sparkling treat that was over far too quickly.

In some ways, I didn't mind too much. I've always seen the world as a hostile place and weather that was relentlessly vile seemed to reassure me that I'd come to the right conclusion. In some ways, it was actually comforting.

But yeah, it was a harsh old Winter. The fields were so sodden that the sheep were sinking up to their knees. The wind was so unflagging that the lawns around the house were hidden beneath a layer of twigs and branches. One of the barn doors had been blown off its hinges. It had been so cold for so long that I shied away from the very thought of going outside unless I absolutely had to. Increasingly I turned my back on the world and spent time on the web.

It became my habit to turn on the Mac even before I boiled a kettle for the first coffee of the day. Five minutes later I'd settle down in front of the screen and see what the Internet had to offer.

And what it had to offer was pretty depressing.

It seemed as if all the algorithms had realised that I took a dismal view of the world and decided that it was their job to back that up and keep me in a little bubble of depression, an echo chamber of my own gloom.

Social algorithms showed me the shallowness of celebrity and that lots and lots of my friends were sharing posts about saving the planet. News-site algorithms showed me, in some considerable statistical detail, just how polluted the world was becoming and how keen celebrities were to raise our awareness of that. Search algorithms just wanted me to worry about pollution, global warming and shallow, over-paid celebrities.

And it was all oddly addictive.

Did you know that we release over one hundred thousand different chemicals into the environment and an increasing number of them aren't water-soluble but will, in fact, start to build up in Ant and Dec's fatty tissue?

Did you know that pollution has become invisible? In the eighties it was a thick column of smoke billowing from a chimney that John Craven could point at and today it's a molecule of mercury, arsenic or cadmium in a mother's breast milk.

Did you know that there are now rivers so polluted that not only can fish not live in them, but if a celebrity fell into the water, say Shane Lynch or Stormzy, they would die?

And I tried not to be too upset by all this, but that didn't really work either because beneath the stupidity and banality, it was upsetting. We seemed hell-bent on poisoning everything as a fall-back plan to making the earth's climate so changed and so challenging that we could no longer survive in it.

After a few months of that, by the time I was standing there with my finger on the button, it really did seem like the only sensible thing to do.

But I am sorry if it didn't turn out so good from your point of view, I really am.

.

Anyway.

Storm Eleanor. She was a beauty. Ninety-plus mile-an-hour winds, driving rain and bitter cold.

She woke me up howling like a jet engine, beating at the air like a Harpy. I swear I thought the windows were about to come in. I turned the pillow over onto the cold side, pulled the duvet over my head and went back to sleep.

In the morning the internet was full of missing roofs, burst riverbanks and droves of concerned celebs. Eleanor had plunged both an Iron Age fort and the last two holes of a links golf course into the raging Atlantic. She had blacked out most of South Wales by toppling a bunch of pylons and she caused chaos at Heathrow, Gatwick and Luton. What a bitch.

So I got to wonder just exactly what she might have done to me.

With my second coffee in hand and snuggled into an

old fleece with a big quilted hood I felt heroic enough to step outside.

It was painfully clear and bright, as sharp and brittle as crystal. Do you know what I mean? When every last particle of dirt and dust has been blown or washed away there's a particular sparkle to the world, a sense of surviving the whirlwind and starting anew. But that cold! Dear Christ, but it was cold. It clawed at my throat and drew a tear from my eye. It was vile and vindictive. As cold as loss, cold as loneliness, cold as the absence of love.

With coffee hugged in both hands I took a walk around. It seemed impossible to believe that Eleanor hadn't ripped a roof off or brought a branch down on a power-line but everything appeared to be in one piece. From the yard I looked out over the fields and saw the sheep watching me with a sort of tentative suspicion. There was the same number of sheep after the storm as there had been before; so all well and good there. I walked up the side of the yard and around the back of the old potting shed, up towards the greenhouses. The ground was strewn with fallen branches and standing water. There were patches of half-drowned grass that looked like paddy and deeper puddles like slivers of a shattered mirror. The greenhouse, however, was in one piece. Not one single broken pane.

But there was something.

Most of the trees on the farm are sycamore or beech but standing on their own, just a hundred yards from the greenhouses, is a pair of what I've always assumed were Douglas firs. Well, they had been a pair. One of them was lying on the ground, all hundred and forty-odd feet of it. She had always seemed a big old tree standing up but, blown over, you could see just how enormous she actually was. And the thing that got me was the way she'd come down. The trunk hadn't broken; she was all in one piece like a toy tree flicked over by a playful finger. Do you remember those model trees that came with train sets and toy soldiers? A brown plastic trunk with rings of green plastic branches circling it and then spreading out at the bottom into a circular base. That was exactly what I was looking at. As the tree had fallen she'd levered up a great circle of ground with her roots. It looked like nothing quite so much as a trap door that had been swung open.

It was hard to imagine what it must have been like when the tree fell, when something that had grown for perhaps a hundred years had given up its life. No one had been here to see. Did it make a sound? Kicking at one of the branches, it flipped over to reveal the dead body of a bird driven inches deep into the muddy ground. A bird killed by a falling tree. That's not something you see every day, is it? The tree's roots were veins ripped from the earth's flesh, some as thick as my thigh, some mere filaments. She had been torn from the bones of the earth. Ripped up by a storm consumed with rage.

In the base of the pit was a hole, a void that didn't seem to make sense. Perhaps it was some animal's burrow, perhaps it was just a hole in the ground but there was something about it that I didn't like the look of.

'Enough of this,' I said to myself, turned on my heel and walked back through the cold to the farm.

·

The following day, this would be the Thursday, was warmer and the warmth brought the mist.

The air was dead still and the clouds were low. A vapour deadened any sound and made everything that wasn't right in front of your nose pale and insubstantial. It was as if I wasn't meant to see too far into the future, as if I was to focus only on the here and now. The further away things were, the harder they were to see; like consequences.

I made coffee but I didn't turn the computer on. The fallen tree had played on my mind all the previous evening and a trace of it had laced my dreams during the night, but I couldn't remember the stuff of those visions, I simply woke feeling that there was a task that needed doing, something that I would rather avoid but wasn't going to get the option to do so. A necessary evil or a painful good.

So what am I telling you? I'm telling you that I don't think it was something that I chose to do. I didn't go looking for this, it came looking for me. Why? I have absolutely no idea. As I get towards the end of my story I wonder about you more. Who are you and where are you? Are you one of many, living a perfect life in the Garden of Eden or are you a sole survivor clinging to a precarious existence? And me? Am I loved or am I loathed? I guess we all want to know that, no matter what our circumstances. No matter what brought us here.

Anyway. That morning.

That morning I threw on some work clothes and grabbed a torch. I suppose I could have told someone what I was doing, I could have asked for help but those ideas seemed far off in the mist and too faint for me to see.

I walked up to the deadfall and the hole it had left in the ground, that wound torn in the earth. It would have been good to have you with me, to have had a hand to hold. The hole in the floor of the pit was even clearer to see in the soft light of an overcast morning. It sucked at that light. It sucked me in. With the torch in my pocket I slid down on my arse till I was at the base of the pit. The edge crumbled and I grabbed one of the bigger roots and held on tight. I braced my feet against the far side of the hole and peered down into the darkness. Whatever was in that space was hard to see, not just unlit, but dim. As if whatever was in the pit wasn't yet sure what it would become.

I pulled the torch from my pocket and turned it on. The beam stabbed down into the depths but showed me hardly anything. And yet, perhaps a few feet down was a thin, cold gleam that slowly became the top rung of a metal ladder disappearing down into darkness. The darkness swirled exactly like the sort of deep water you always tried to avoid finding yourself in.

Are you still with me?

I knew that ladder would either hold me or it wouldn't; that when I launched my feet out into the murk I was committed to a course of action that I didn't fully understand and didn't truly want. So, I jumped, or rather, I let myself fall.

My feet landed on the ladder.

I clung to the root that was still in one hand, reached down to get my other hand on a rung. I cried out but no one heard. Of course, I dropped the torch. It fell like a star tumbling into a well. What could I do but follow it?

The metal ladder was cold and thin. It was like climbing down a rusty blade. And I hate heights. One foot reached down, feeling for the next rung. I slid my hand down the stringer. My foot found the next rung and I had to see if it would take my weight. Like a broken wooden monkey I worked my way down the stick.

There was condensation on the ladder. It was damp. Cold and damp.

What did I say about 'cold and damp' not being a precipice that you could fall off, not being something that induced fear? Seems I was wrong. I've been wrong a lot in the last few days.

Down a step. Another.

The ladder became a column of bones, a spinal cord that clicked and clacked as I wormed my way down it. It became an umbilicus joining my life to this earthy womb.

At last, ground beneath my feet. I was down.

I held my hands out and slowly swung from left to right, feeling nothing. I looked up, one single star. A pinprick of light. A mote. When I closed my eyes, I could see more. I could see a handful of dots that moved in rhythmic waves and as they swayed from side to side they multiplied. I began to believe that I could see them through my tightly shut lids and they increased, reproduced and grew in number. They became the phosphorescence that plays in the sluggish waves of the sea at night. The swirling galaxy that dances alone and lifeless at either end of time.

I sank to my knees and that's when I found it. My hands closed around a shape that was as changeable and unformed as the darkness, as fluid as the eddying motes in my eye.

I slipped it into my pocket, turned and began the precarious climb to the surface.

.

The end.

Or the beginning.

Either way, we are at that point now.

I can't remember a thing about the climb or how I managed to pull myself up that last few feet and get out of the hole. I can barely remember staggering back to the farmhouse like a drunk, my feet falling flat and heavy on the muddy ground. I can't remember getting indoors or what I did then but all these things must have happened because I woke from an oblivious sleep naked in my bed. The world was very quiet and a little daylight slipped past the curtains. I'd slept the clock around. Memory came back to me like bubbles rising to a surface. I pulled on some clothes and went downstairs.

The Mac was still on, its fan humming.

On the table in front of it, my jacket was covering an object about the size of two clenched fists. I lifted up a corner to take a look before letting it fall back in place.

I went through into the kitchen and poured a big slug of whisky into a dirty glass. It tasted harsh like a medicine, an anaesthetic, perhaps.

And then I opened a Word file on the computer and wrote this, this document that you are reading. My testament. My record of what I have done and what, at last, I will do.

My jacket is lying on the floor and the object is sitting on my desk. It has decided what it wants to be seen as. I was thinking that if this had happened hundreds of years ago, it might look like a Shaman's bag of bones or a witch's fetish. But then I realised that this couldn't have happened that far back in the past, we hadn't wounded the Earth back then, she didn't need this.

And yes, of course I've wondered if I have lost my mind. I don't think so. But the way to find out is to press the button and see what happens. That's the only way really.

So here I am, reluctant eco-warrior with his finger on the nuclear trigger. I think that while I slept, the object absorbed its environment like a chameleon blending in. But it didn't want to hide. It wanted to make its purpose as clear as possible. And to my mind, it has. The whisky is finished now. On the desk is an empty glass and a small box with a button on it and on that button is clearly marked Restore to Default Settings. And I think about the warm dark earth that I plucked the object from and I think about the world we live in and the path we seem to have set ourselves on. Save the planet? Well maybe I will. Does it mean what it says?

Restore to Default Settings.

Everything? Could it? Should I?

I'm sorry, but I think I might just push it. I think it might be best if I did.

I hope this turns out well.

Here goefnivdfs'obdfgmsp\nbokfd b m;/.km/.   ich;q
I   '/////

WEED

A WHITE arrow painted on the road.

Gorse like wind-blown spume on the crest of a hedge.

A buzzard soaring against the pale blue sky.

Traffic. A long, long line of traffic following a slow and muddy tractor.

A cabbage field with perfectly regular rows of perfectly regular brassica, fat glossy and green.

Ben had heard about something called "mindfulness" on the radio yesterday. It was supposed to be a way of not dwelling on the past or worrying about the future and Ben had such a lot of past and such a lot of future to dwell on and worry about that he'd decided to give it a go. It seemed to be just making lists of stuff that you could see as and when you saw it but the woman on the radio had said that it grounded you in the here and now and that was good for you. Good for your wellbeing, or something. Ben thought that was what she'd said. It didn't seem to be making much of a difference yet. Perhaps it took time?

A stop sign and a junction.

An oncoming car.

Oops.

Ben stood on the brakes and the van slid to a halt. The guy in the Peugeot gave him the finger as he shot past. Ben took a breath. He looked left, he looked right, he looked in the van's mirrors; there was nothing else around. He knocked her into gear and slowly crossed the junction. Perhaps he should spend a bit more effort concentrating and a bit less on being mindful? The van picked up speed, creaking and rattling as she did so.

About a mile further on Ben took a left down a long, narrow lane that led to Little Pendene. It was a typical country lane, two tracks of grey potholed dirt with a Mohican of grass running down the middle. This grass had grown longer than most as the lane didn't see much traffic, the stalks and stems played a twanging little tune on the under body of the van as he bumped along. David drove a Range Rover and Anne had a Hi Lux so Ben supposed neither of them noticed the grass.

He pulled up at the gate. Got out of the van, the door grumbling on its corroded hinge. He threw the latch and swung the big farm gate open; heard the dogs bark the very moment the gate started to move.

'Yeah, yeah. Shut the fuck up,' he mumbled under his breath, but when he saw Anne waving to him from the kitchen he let a big smile light up his face and waved enthusiastically back.

The dogs ran towards him scattering the gravel on the sweeping drive. A retired racing dog, as thin and grey a hound as a piece of chewed-up string, and some sort of terrier with all the noisy aggression of the shortest person at the bar on a Saturday night. Ben had heard their names a hundred times but hadn't yet bothered to remember them.

He'd only been coming here once a week for the last two years.

Ben jumped back in the van and pulled onto the drive; parked her there. By the time he had the gate closed and latched again the dogs had realised that, bark as they might, this human had once again invaded their patch and wasn't going away. Some battles you just couldn't win it seemed, and they wandered off to patrol the rest of their empire.

'Hi,' beamed Anne. 'Have you brought your strimmer? Of course you have. There's always strimming that needs doing. It's in the van, isn't it?'

'Hello,' said Ben. 'How are you? Weather's been good, eh?'

They stood and smiled at each other for a moment. Ben, a big hard slab of a man and Anne, jodhpurs and a fleece packed full of soft curves and generous swellings. Ben blinked first.

'So,' he said. 'What do you want doing? The walled garden could do with a tidy and stuff in the round bed needs cutting back.'

'David's left a list,' she said. She patted her pocket on her hip but no list appeared. 'Can you strim down by the pond, cut the hedge by the stables and there are some new plants he's bought that need potting on. They're in the conservatory.'

'Ooh,' said Ben. 'What's he got?'

'I'll show you,' and she turned and walked up the drive. Ben waited a beat before he followed her so that he could watch her ass roll as she walked.

David and Anne's conservatory was an ornate, mono-pitch affair built against the south-facing wall of the walled garden. Its glass panes were cut with fish-scale bottoms and leaded in with actual lead. The gables were decorated and carved and the back wall was un-plastered brick that had been lime washed. David was a stickler for the details.

On the staging against the back wall was a big parcel that had been partially unwrapped. Layers and layers of blue, industrial cling-film had been torn away and inside were plastic seed trays, bags of bare rootstock and some seedlings coming on under transparent plastic covers. The outside of the parcel was covered in bar codes and posting stickers in Chinese characters as well as English.

'He got them on the internet.'

'I always like to see what I'm getting.'

'Well, you can't get these that way, apparently. They're rare and exotic or some new hybrids or something. He's quite excited so you better make sure everything grows.'

Ben looked at her and smiled. 'Ben Plant, professional gardener at your service, ma'am.'

She winced. 'There are instructions in here somewhere,' said Anne as she rummaged in the parcel.

'Better not lose them then, eh,' said Ben.

Anne left him to it and after ten minutes or so Ben had the whole parcel undone and spread out on the staging.

特注 意 些危 的植物 said one of the enclosed leaflets in bold red lettering. That's good to know, thought Ben and he wondered what it meant. There were instructions on soil types and planting depths that had been translated from Chinese into something very similar to English but their real meaning had been buried in the process. There were some basic diagrams that appeared to explain which plants liked full sun and which were shade-tolerant, how big they might grow and, for the bulbs, how deep to plant them, but what each plant was, was harder to tell. Ben carefully folded up the paperwork and put it in his pocket.

Well, he thought, they're plants. Stick 'em in some soil and give 'em some water and they've got two chances as my old gaffer used to say; slim and none.

.

An angry sky darkening with bruise-coloured clouds.

A track that twists and turns through the woods.

Autumn beech leaves paving the ground with gold.

The van's headlights, showing the way.

A caravan. A container. My home.

Thought Ben, being mindful.

He drove the Vito into the clearing and parked her up by the container. It would have been nice if a dog had come bounding out of the dark to greet him or a light had been shining in the window of the caravan. There could have been a voice, perhaps, shouting a hello, or smoke curling from the log-burner's chimney. None of that, thought Ben. None of that.

The caravan's door was unlocked. He had very little worth stealing and very few people around here would be stupid enough to steal from him. He turned on a light, an LED that ran off the battery. He knelt before the wood burner and started a fire. He'd gutted the big caravan when he'd first moved it here and now it had a plywood floor and the stove, a kitchen-living space that had an ancient butcher-block table and a saggy sofa. A solar panel and a turbine charged the old submarine batteries. An iMac squatted in one corner, a gas cooker in the other. A bed. A shower. When you actually thought about what you needed, you found the list of things and stuff wasn't very long. What you actually needed in a home was a lover or a friend but none of that here, thought Ben. None of that.

He closed the door behind him.

And after a time the greasy black casserole, full of yesterday's stew, was warming on the stove. In the wood burner, fire sprites danced along the split limbs of a beech that had come down earlier in the year; they cackled as they turned the wood into heat and ash. Ben had a chipped glass full of Malbec in his hand and outside he could hear the last few birds telling each other bedtime stories.

After he'd eaten and splashed a little more wine into the glass, in order to see if he could find out more about David's new plants, he started to go through his books. From junk shops and bookshops, car boots and charity bring'n'buys he'd put together a library that ranged from 70's glossy paperbacks to leather-bound tomes illustrated with hand-tinted etchings. Books on gardening and books on plants, there was something tactile about them, turning the pages was like getting your hands into the soil. Digging through the book pile he eventually found mention of a few of the plants in the parcel. There was a rare cultivar of Meconopsis that promised a poppy-like flower of such dark a blue that it was almost black. A Chinese tulip tree, but not a species that any of Ben's books could identify and something that looked like Yunnan meadow-rue, but the paperwork that came with the plants seemed to suggest that David's specimen would grow far bigger than normal.

They certainly weren't common plants; in fact, they were so unusual that Ben was surprised that they weren't on a protected list. Countries tended to dislike having their native flora pillaged by foreigners and none more so than China especially after the British stole tea from them a couple of hundred years ago. One of the books had a good chapter on the perils of plant hunting. There was Robert Fortune who stole the tea, Seibold, who stole the flowering cherry from Japan and so was tried for high treason and George Forrest who collected thousands of plants from China and only just escaped after the rest of his party were killed. Plants were a serious business.

A pair of owls hooted outside.

Flame rolled in the wood burner.

Ben remembered what it was like to be in a foreign country with people keen to kill you.

Damn. That was just the sort of thing this mindfulness was meant to avoid.

·

The wipers squeaked as they went back and forth across the windscreen. The potholes in the lane were now puddles. When he got to the farm gate the two dogs just looked at him from the warmth of their basket just inside the porch.

Getting out of the van, Ben felt raindrops sneak between his hat and his collar to run cold fingertips down his neck. Gusts of wind slapped the rain into his face. Individual drops pecked at his waxed jacket like a flock of tiny, angry birds. Water was already standing on the drive and the gutters were running full tilt. Ben splashed across the gravel and stood by the open porch door. He didn't bother to knock. The little dog set up a steady and constant bark. The old greyhound just watched him out of one rheumy eye. Ben sneered at them as a blocked gutter dripped on to his shoulder.

'I suppose it's too wet to mow the lawns, is it?' said

Anne as she came barrelling down the corridor.

'A bit.'

'Too wet to spray weed killer on the drive?'

'Yep.'

'Well we better find something for you to do.'

Ben smiled to himself but said, 'I'll tidy the walled garden. It'll be sheltered from the worst of it in there.'

'Alright,' said Anne. 'And weed the veg garden and David saw some brambles on the back hedge. We don't like brambles. Or nettles.'

Ben nodded. Like it was an easy thing to keep almost two acres of garden free of brambles, nettles and weeds; invasive little buggers that they all were. 'I know,' he said. 'I know.' Anne disappeared back into the warm and Ben walked back into the wet to get some tools from the van.

The garden at Little Pendene had been laid out by David and Anne when they bought the old farm, renovated the farmhouse and added a stable block and a walled garden. Architectural salvage and a healthy budget meant that everything now looked as if it had been here forever. The garden was divided into a formal section, the veg garden, an orchard, the hedged garden, a walled garden and the pond. There was a thick laurel hedge that sheltered the whole place from the prevailing winds and the pillars and columns of mature trees supported a leafy canopy over the entire garden.

Over the couple of years that he'd been working there, Ben had come to feel that the garden belonged to him and that it would all be much, much better if they simply let him get on with it but he also understood that being told what to do was in the nature of employment, and a little bit like the military chain of command.

With a barrow, secateurs, loppers, a rake and a spade, Ben marched off through the deluge to the walled garden. This room of the garden was easily Ben's favourite. That extra bit of shelter meant that it could be planted up with exotics as well as roses, that fruit trees could be trained against the walls and that everything that was grown in here seemed to enjoy a longer season, but, for most things, that season was coming to an end now and Ben filled barrow after barrow with cuttings, trimmings and swept-up leaves.

And it rained. Rain bounced off the conservatory roof, it beat across Ben's broad back and splashed across the stone pavers and the gravel. After an hour Ben took his flask and stepped into the shelter of the conservatory. He poured a steaming mug of coffee and slumped down on a wooden bench. As he looked around, he saw the plants that he had potted on just last week.

The black plastic pots were in orderly rows against the wall and across the stone floor of the conservatory. Two and a half litre pots of rich, dark compost topped with handfuls of fine grit. From almost all of the pots a bit of something green was sprouting or prospering or hanging grimly on to life. Two chances, slim and none; and most of the plants seemed to have grasped at the slim one.

There was one rather strange exception, to Ben's eye. A half-dozen or more of the pots sprouted what appeared to be a feeble and diseased sort of vine or ivy. Whatever it was, it was tumbling over the pot edges, falling to the floor and then growing off in tendrils and runners of sickly pink and ash grey. Ben had no idea what it was but as all the pots that it was growing in also sprouted something recognisable, he guessed that it wasn't what was actually meant to be growing there.

Perhaps it was a weed, but it was no weed that Ben had ever seen before. He reached out and hooked his finger under one of the tendrils and then squeaked out loud as he snatched it back. 'Bastard,' he growled. It had stung him. Stung him and left a red welt on his finger.

Well, he thought, they can be someone else's problem.

But of course, they weren't.

.

The next few Thursdays saw Ben kept busy.

A garden, they say, isn't something that you have; it's something that you do. Gardens leak upwards into the sky, was another of Ben's favourites, and all the better for being true. Ben liked brambles, nettles and weeds, he liked lawns that had grown too long and hedges that had grown too tall because, for him, it all meant money. It all meant work.

He cut the hedges straight and true and checked his work with a spirit level, because he was pretty sure that David did.

Wearing a tall pair of wellies, he dredged the stream that ran through the garden and fed the pond because it had become choked with weed.

He prowled around the garden, strimmer in hand, like some rapacious beast searching out every last clump of dock weed and tangle of convolvulus, but it always seemed that whatever he strimmed flat came back twice as enthusiastically. And that was good for business too.

This particular Autumn-fresh afternoon, David came stomping down through the garden to find him. David liked to dress as if he was a country squire, corduroy trousers and a tweed jacket that appeared to be made from wire wool. He had a paper sack full of bulbs in one hand and a mug of tea in the other.

Just the bulbs, it turned out, were for Ben.

'Plant these in under the trees and in that bed by the sundial, could you?' and Ben said that he could.

'It's not looking too bad, for the time of year,' said David looking around the garden. Ben smiled. 'Could you dig over one of the raised beds in the walled garden and could you prepare some of the bed beside the house where we dug that fuchsia up. I want most of those new plants going out there in the spring.'

'Oh. OK.'

'Speaking of the new arrivals, have you seen what seems to have hitchhiked a ride in with them?'

'I saw something a couple of weeks ago. I've not been in there for a while. That sort of vine thing?'

'Yeah. I think it's weird and I want it gone,' he said. 'Sling it all on the bonfire, will you.'

Ben nodded. 'What do you think it is?' he asked.

'I think it's a weed,' said David. 'You know what a weed is, don't you?'

Ben laughed.

'A weed is a plant that wants to grow where people want something else,' Ben and David said in unison.

'There's another good one, you know,' said Ben. David raised his eyebrows and Ben said, 'A weed is a plant that has mastered every survival skill except for learning how to grow in rows.'

'Ooh, I like that,' said David. 'Let's see if this can survive being dug up and burnt, shall we?'

Ben got his tools together and they both walked over to the walled garden. It had only been a couple of weeks since he was last here but, as soon as he stepped through the door and into the garden, he could see what had rattled Dave. Even from outside the conservatory, he could see twists and tendrils of grey leaves and pinky-red stems climbing up the rear wall of the conservatory and scrabbling up the glass in the front.

'Wow,' said Ben.

'What do you think it is?' asked David.

'Dunno,' said Ben peering through the glass as if he was watching tigers at the zoo.

'It's not Japanese knot weed, is it?'

'No. That's totally different and it doesn't grow particularly fast.'

'Well,' said David. 'Let's get it on the bonfire before we see what else it can do. Look, it's got bloody flowers on it,' and sure enough there were a few little splashes of colour at the tips of the stems climbing the back wall.

'Shall I keep...'

'No,' said David. He patted Ben on the back, emptied the dregs of his tea on the ground and walked back to the house.

Ben pushed at the conservatory door but it stuck half way and he saw that there was a mat of tendrils on the floor, jamming the door. He knelt down thinking to pull them out of the way and then just in time remembered how he had been stung. Worse than a bloody nettle, he thought to himself and pulled his gloves out of his pocket.

It took him half an hour to get all of the creeping vine out of the conservatory and out of the pots. In a couple of the plant pots, the vine's roots were so entangled with whatever was meant to be growing in there that he had to give up and sling the whole thing, pot and all, into the barrow. The vine's roots turned out to be a bright and angry red and so easy to spot but one bit of rootstock got past the cuff of his glove and Ben discovered that the roots themselves secreted some sort of irritant as well. The flowers were small red and yellow bracts that were sticky and had a clump of hard pods at their base.

Stem, root, leaf and flower; Ben bundled almost all of it up into a great pile overflowing the barrow and then squeezed out between the raised beds, through the garden gate and off towards the bonfire.

He kept one of the plants for himself, some root and a few tendrils in a plant pot that he put in the back of his van. It was always interesting to discover new plants and see what they did.

·

Beech trees in the wood; their tall straight trunks make a barcode.

His van's cab, unloved and filthy with mud and mess, dirt and cobwebs.

Wood pigeons fluttering aimlessly in the canopy overhead.

The twists and turns of the track, like his story leading to how and where he now lives.

A figure in the woods?

A threat?

No. But there could be. There could be.

Sometimes Ben sees danger everywhere. Everything poses a threat or appears to be a potential risk. It doesn't make him jumpy. It makes him very slow and cautious. It makes him pointlessly careful. He's just come back from working in a garden in St Agnes. He worried a lot while he was there. Would he slip on the steps and break his hip? Would the chainsaw kick back and turn his arm to hamburger? Would the strimmer pick up a stone and fling it into his eye? He had to force himself to keep on working. At the end of the day, it had been a struggle to load up the van and drive home. At every junction in the road he imagined he heard the squeal of brakes and the hollow slam of metal crashing together, crushing bone and flesh like a cruel, cold hand. He knew what his blood would taste like and how high-pitched his scream would be. He drove slowly and carefully all the way home and absolutely nothing at all happened but he was still scared the entire bloody way. Now he was home. Parked up by the container. Looking at his caravan. Feeling scared.

It's nothing. It's nothing. It's nothing, he thought.

After a while his breathing got easier, his pulse slowed and his heart got out of his mouth and went back to live behind his ribs. He breathed out and he felt the tension fall from his shoulders. He opened the van door and winced as the corroded hinge squeaked.

This hadn't been a good day, he thought, but it hadn't been a bad one either. Sometimes the PTSD left him paralysed, literally unable to move. Those were bad days. This hadn't been a bad day.

In the caravan he kicked his boots off and emptied the last of his flask into a coffee cup. He yawned and rubbed his fingers through the crisp curls of his beard. With a handful of sticks and a firelighter he set the log burner going and then he turned on the iMac. Scrumpled up beside the sagging sofa, he found the paperwork from the parcel of plants. He started putting words from there into

Google; plant names, the name of the shipper, something that appeared to be a company name. The log burner was providing a red-gold glow by the time the Internet was offering what might be some useful hits.

What seemed to be most likely was that David had bought the plants from a seller in China who was offering rare stuff on eBay. Some of the plants that David had bought were featured on the seller's eBay Store, but a lot of the stuff wasn't. There was a bit of Pidgin English suggesting that you contact the seller if you had any specific wants or needs.

That was kind of weird, thought Ben. It almost seemed to be offering plants on demand. He imagined wizened Chinese gardeners with faces like philosophers, bent backs and bamboo rakes tending the seedlings. More likely to be hydroponics, he thought, and that reminded him. He had a job to do before suppertime.

Ben looked out of the window. It had gone still and dark outside. Not so much like the presence of night, more of an absence. As if the day had gone truant, had taken the opportunity to slip away while his attention was elsewhere. Outside of the caravan was a black and empty space, but pretty much anything could be hiding in it.

'No,' he said and shook his head. 'There's nothing to fear but fear itself,' he said under his breath. 'Nothing but fear itself.'

He picked up a bunch of keys and his Maglite, pushed his feet into a pair of beaten-up Crocs. Outside, he walked over to the container and undid the big Krieg lock that kept the doors closed shut. Just inside the doors was a black plastic curtain that stopped any light spilling out into the wood, but the smell in the air was very distinctive. It was warm and moist and oh so sweet. Ben closed the doors behind him before stepping through the curtain. The rest of the container was lit by grow lights hanging from the ceiling. The floor was full of old pallets on top of which were plants in drums being fed by a complicated network of pipes and guttering that crawled over staging and wound its way across scaffolding trestles. The air was so humid it was almost un-breathable. The smell was intoxicatingly sweet. There was the sound of running water and the whine of small pumps. The plants seemed to be thriving; distinctive serrated blade shaped leaves and dense racemes of sticky bud.

The container was full of weed, or Cannabis sativa, as it would be more properly called. Ben started to make sure that it was all growing as well as it could.

.

People think that gardens lie dormant in the Winter but they don't and certainly gardeners don't. If you own a garden, you might choose to ignore it for two or three months but if you earn part of your living from being a gardener then you pretty much make sure your boots are sturdy, that you have a good hat, some dry gloves and that you're wearing plenty of layers. Then you get in your van and you drive off to work.

In the winter you can see the structure of a garden, the bones of the thing. Ben pruned some of the smaller trees and bigger shrubs at Little Pendene, getting them in better shape for the spring. He swept up all the fallen leaves. The following week he swept up all the leaves again. Then next week he did that again. He dug over the veg garden. He pruned the orchard making each apple tree a goblet shape. He pressure-washed the patio and burnt the bonfire.

Ben liked the Winter. The slower pace of life suited him. He saw fewer people and that eased his stress and anxiety attacks. He loved the colours, the mustard yellows and pale greens, the vibrant reds and flamboyant oranges; phoenix feathers caught in the black web of bare branched trees. He liked to watch the rooks being blown across the sky like dead leaves. He liked to listen to the wind and the rain while, preferably, not being in the wind and the rain. Winter suited him.

Anne and David were less to be seen over those months. Some weeks she'd be there, tending to her horses, and they would chat for a time. Some weeks he'd be there and the two men would walk down to the pond to discuss planting schemes for the water margin or walk the paddock looking for any ragwort or cowbane that, if it were left, would poison the horses. Anne was sensibly paranoid about her animals and she would allow no yew or privet anywhere on the property. Nature could be vicious.

For himself, Ben hibernated as much as he could. He tried to only do what he had to, or what he enjoyed. Apart from Anne and David's garden, which he visited every Thursday, he did just enough work to balance the books. He brought one crop of weed in just before Christmas and sold it to his usual contact. He swung an axe to split logs for the stove. He peddled his old mountain bike into the village to get the shopping. He cleaned out the grow room and got another crop started. He read books. He stared out into the woods trying to breathe deeply but think not at all. The plant pot with the red-stemmed vine in it sat behind the container and Ben forgot all about it.

.

The weather was warmer, the sky was brighter, the days were longer and things began to grow again. It would take a few weeks for the soil to start to warm up before things began to germinate, thought Ben but there he proved to be wrong.

The bonfire had blossomed.

Tucked away in one corner of the garden, it may well have been missed at first but now it was all too obvious that burning the vine hadn't had the desired effect. The fire had reduced the bonfire down to a pile of ash but now that grey desert had bloomed. Red tendrils, grey leaves; disturbingly appropriate for where it was growing and somehow the simple fact of the growth was disturbing in itself.

'I've never seen anything like it,' said David, his hands thrust deep into his pockets, his cordovan brogues safely outside the circle of cinders and mud.

'Nor me,' said Ben. 'Nor me.'

The vine had made a low pile of growth in the middle of the circle of the fire, a mound of twisting, curling vine upon vine. A few thicker tree branches and a couple of metal fence posts had been left by the fire sticking up from the ashes and the vine had climbed these enthusiastically. The growing tips of each strand of vine were thin and delicate but curled like grasping fingers. The grey leaves formed dense bunches of foliage. Red-stemmed runners spread out along the ground radiating from the central clump of growth. In the centre of the plant, some of the older vines were starting to thicken and become woody.

'I don't like the looks of that,' said David reaching down towards one of the nodes on a runner. Ben stopped him, explained that the plant stung to the touch.

David laughed. 'Really? I'm surprised every garden doesn't have some of this,' and he shook his head in annoyance. 'Look,' he said prodding at the node with a stick. 'It's rooting. Runners and roots, just like a bramble and you know what those buggers can be like.'

'Damn right,' said Ben.

'But we burnt it. You ripped it up and burnt it. How can it be growing?'

Ben shrugged. Rubbed at his greying beard. Squinted at the problem.

'There are plants that can survive fires. Hell, some plants need to go through a fire before their seeds can germinate. I don't know. I don't know what it is. Do you?'

David hunched his shoulders and kicked at the ground. 'What's' that?' he said. 'Over at the back.'

Ben took a step to his right and tilted his head, dipped his chin when he recognised what the dark blur, half buried in the vine was. 'Dead bird,' he said. 'Just a bird.'

David sucked at his teeth. 'Strim it,' he said.

'I don't know that that's such a great...'

'Just do it, will you,' and David stomped off up the garden.

.

'Dipsy's dead,' said Anne, the moment Ben stepped out of his van.

Who the fuck is Dipsy, he thought to himself while letting his face slip into a look of mild concern.

'I thought that she'd eaten something or that it was old age. It started on Friday. It was like she couldn't breathe and then I saw all these swellings around her eyes and nose and I just though, oh God, what's wrong with her and then Widdle got sick too.'

Dipsy and Widdle, thought Ben. It's the dogs, she's talking about the dogs. Sure enough the little terrier was sitting alone in its basket with one of those big plastic shields around its neck. Its face looked red and puffy.

'Oh no,' he said. 'That's awful.'

'The vet didn't know what it was. We haven't changed their food or anything. I guess they might have been poisoned but who would do something like that? David said it might have been burglars wanting to shut the dogs up but I think he's watched too many movies. That's just silly, don't you think?'

Ben was turning the first thought that had jumped into his head over and over in his mind. It's that plant, he thought. It's that fucking plant.

'Ben?' said Anne. She was looking at him, her hands squarely on her hips and her head cocked to one side, her chest rising and falling. 'Ben?'

'Yeah. No, I mean, that's awful. Poor you. Poor…'

'Dipsy.'

'Yeah. Poor Dipsy.'

'What do you think happened?' she asked. 'What do you think did it to her?'

Alkaloids, thought Ben but what he said was, "I have no idea.'

David emerged from the house; all checked shirt, knitted tie and outrage. 'People are disgusting, aren't they?' he growled. 'I mean, the dogs have never harmed anyone. John's coming this afternoon. You know, John? The electrician. He's putting in two more security cameras. Not that it'll do you any good, eh,' and he patted the terrier's back. It gave a pitiable little whine. David crooked his finger at Ben like a diner calling a waiter. 'Come with me,' he said. 'We've got another problem.'

After ten minutes walking around the garden it was clear what the problem was.

'That bloody vine has got everywhere. I can't believe how quick it's growing. I can't believe how it's spreading.'

Although it was all new growth, a layer of vine once again covered the ash of the bonfire. Where the strimmer had spat bits of shredded tendril out, those bits had, as Ben had feared, started to root and there were dozens of tiny runners and small grey leaves for fifteen feet or more around the bonfire.

'Look at this,' said David pulling Ben off towards the walled garden. 'I think you missed a bit.'

The conservatory was literally exploding with growth. The vine had pushed up against, and in some places through, the glass. It had broken out through the ventilation panels and was crawling across the roof and up the wall at the back. It climbed every single wooden beam and then hung down in long strands from roof to floor. Poisonously pink and red stemmed, thick grey foliage and grasping tendrils, the conservatory was bursting with something that should no longer have been there.

'I, um. I thought I got it…'

'Obviously not,' said David.

'Nobody's been in since?'

'No. Oh, I'm sorry. Is this our fault? Should we go around and check up on you? Should we have made sure that what you were asked to do actually got done?'

'David!' snapped Anne from behind them. 'It isn't Ben's

fault.'

David sighed. 'I'm sorry. It's just, all a bit much what with the dogs as well. Have you got any weed killer with you?'

'Yeah,' said Ben.

'What have you got?'

'Glyphosate.'

'That's like Roundup, yeah.'

'Same stuff, but it's concentrated. Dilute to taste, as it were.'

'Spray that,' said David pointing at the greenhouse. 'Drench it.'

'I can't spray the whole garden and it's spreading everywhere.'

'If the spray takes it down, we can paint it on the leaves. At least we'll have a plan.'

.

On the Wednesday, Ben's phone rang. 'It's David,' said David.

'Hi.'

'Umm. How long does that weed killer normally take to work then?'

'Why? I put it on pretty strong. It might all take another week or two to die back completely but it should be showing the effects.'

'Have you got anything stronger?'

'No. That's pretty much all you can get these days. Why?'

'Well, it hasn't done much. In fact, it hasn't done anything,' and Ben heard David growl in frustration. 'And the dog died. Widdle died.'

'Right,' said Ben. 'I'm sorry.'

'Anne's dog really, said David. 'I'll see you tomorrow,' and he rang off.

Ben put the phone down on the sofa next to him. He stared blankly out of the window at the trees in the wood. He listened to his own breathing. He listened to the wood burner as it ticked. He filled the moka pot with water and grounds and put it on the top of the stove, partly because he wanted a coffee, partly for the distraction from listening to his own thoughts as they ran around and around, like a Ferris wheel without a break.

They hadn't joined the dots yet, he thought. They hadn't realised that the plant was poisonous, well, deadly if you were a dog or a bird. He'd bet the dead bird in the bonfire had eaten some part of the vine. And it stung. And it was Roundup resistant. Oh crap, he thought. The penny dropped. Glyphosate resistant. It wasn't some weird exotic from China that had hitchhiked all the way over here by accident. The damn thing was engineered. It was a GMO. A fuckin' GMO.

The moka pot hissed and the caravan filled with the smell of fresh coffee.

He pulled up a stool in front of the iMac and flicked the machine on.

The listings that he'd previously found weren't on eBay anymore and when he looked for the seller's page, that wasn't there either. He looked in his browser history for some of the pages that he'd looked at last time but they wouldn't load. They'd been taken down. OK. That was weird.

There were only two reasons for weird stuff to happen

in Ben's opinion, cock-up or conspiracy, and Chinese eBay dealers who had a buck, or a renminbi, to make didn't let their websites crash. So what was the conspiracy, he wondered?

Getting news out of China was about as easy as getting rare plants out used to be. Searching the web for stories about GMOs in China was as fruitful as Robert Fortune would have been if he had asked the Emperor and the mandarins if he could just have the secret of tea to take away with him.

But there was something.

According to CNN, Beijing had imposed a quarantine and exclusion zone in one of the central provinces in an attempt to halt a swine-fever crisis. All movement in and out of the area was banned plus there was a news blackout covering the area. Well, fine, but this particular province was a long way from other swine-fever outbreaks. Why the news blackout over a bunch of pigs? At the dead centre of the quarantine zone was where the eBay seller's nursery was supposed to be.

'Conspiracy,' said Ben to himself. He drained the last of the cold coffee. 'It's a conspiracy.'

·

A murder of crows flying rag-tag across an ice-blue sky.

A spider spinning its web on the dashboard by the A-pillar, laying a trap.

Road works, barriers and striped cones around a hazard, a hole, a danger.

Ben was being mindful; the problem was that the peril seemed to be with him in the here and now.

The Vito bounced down the lane. Its suspension creaking and from the back of the van there was a clattering and a bang as Ben's tools slid around. Ben rocked around on his seat as if he was the captain of a tiny ship caught on a stormy sea. A couple of his gardening books sat on the passenger seat next to him.

When he got to Little Pendene, he found that the gate was wide open. No dogs to keep in any more, he supposed. The gravel on the drive crunched beneath his wheels. He saw David and Anne through the kitchen window. It looked as if they were shouting at each other. Ben sighed and turned the engine off. David arrived at the driver's door and Ben wound the window down.

'Hey,' said Ben.

'This is a pretty pickle, isn't it,' said David. He looked harassed. Ben had never seen David looking harassed before.

Ben patted the books. 'I've got some ideas,' he said.

'They better be good ideas. Come and have a look.'

The two men marched off down the garden but the problem could be seen almost immediately. The walled garden had disappeared. Where it had stood, where it still stood, was just a mountain of vine. Ben could still roughly see the shape but not one inch of wall or coping tile or doorway was visible through the dense mat of vine, tendril and leaf.

'Fuck,' said Ben.

'Fuck, indeed,' said David. 'I can't believe it. I'm looking at it but I still can't believe it.'

Ben swallowed. He felt the anxiety start to build in him.

'And,' said David, looking at Ben. 'Mister Gardener Man. What are your ideas? What is it? How is it growing this fast?'

Ben took a deep breath. 'Well, it's hard to tell how fast it's growing…'

'No it fuckin' isn't,' squeaked David. 'You can practically watch it.'

'OK. OK. There are bamboos that grow like three feet a day.'

'That isn't bamboo.'

'Kudzu grows really fast.'

'Doesn't look anything like this.'

'I know.'

'Oh god, here she comes,' said David under his breath and Ben turned to see Anne running down the lawn. Her hair was wild. It was obvious that she'd been crying. 'Tell him, Ben. Tell him we need to call someone. Tell him we need to call the police or someone like that.'

'Well,' said Ben. 'It would be DEFRA if we called anybody.'

'No,' snapped David. 'For the twentieth time, no.'

'Why not?' said Ben furrowing his brow and tugging at his beard.

'I'll show you,' and David led them down towards the pond.

The pond was big. It was about forty feet across but only near the very centre was water still visible. The rest of the surface, the margins and the edges and the banks that led down to it were covered in vine, sprawling, spreading and invasive, thick and choking vine. The vine had climbed the trees near the pond's edge and they had completely disappeared beneath the dense growth. There was a line of pink stem and grey leaf that followed the line of the stream that flowed out of the pond and into the neighbouring farmer's field.

'Ah,' said Ben.

'What?' said Anne. 'That's just more reason to let people know, isn't it?'

'What's the maximum penalty?' asked David.

Ben thought for a moment. 'Five thousand pound fine or two to three years. That would be for a serious case.'

David just raised his eyebrows.

'What are you talking about?' said Anne.

'It was aimed at stopping Japanese knotweed but there's legislation about letting an invasive species invade some else's property. Jail or a fine, or both.'

'I can't believe this,' muttered David. Anne seemed speechless.

'How did you find those plants? Did you talk to anyone at the other end? I mean, they were some rare old things. And this,' and Ben shrugged looking at the rampant vine.

David sank down on to his haunches. 'I was just looking for interesting stuff. You know, something a bit different. Some of the things that they were offering on eBay, they were so rare that there was literally no mention of those varieties anywhere else. Not in the books, not on the web.' David picked up a stone and threw it into the pond. It disappeared under the vine, silently and without a trace. 'So I emailed them. They were cagey at first but I let them think that my first order was just a sort of sample. That if I was happy then there would be some big money going their way.'

'What was all that about? Why? Why did you…?' Anne just stopped and shook her head. Ben played with his beard.

'Eventually they came clean. Told me what they were

doing. They were inventing things. They weren't selling rare varieties; these were totally new, gene-spliced, never been seen before in any garden varieties.'

'GMO,' muttered Ben.

'Exactly.'

'What?' said Anne.

'GMO. Genetically modified organism. Mutated. Engineered. Man-made.'

David nodded. 'But how does that explain this?'

'You weren't supposed to get this,' said Ben. 'The other plants, yes. But not this. This escaped. There was a mix up, an error. Something. Because I think this is doing exactly what it's meant to do. I think this is military.'

David looked up and frowned.

'I think this is weaponised. A little experiment that was all too successful.'

'What are you talking about,' said Anne.

'I think this is effectively, grow-your-own barbed wire. There is no reason in nature that I can think of for it to be as vicious as this.'

'Vicious? What do you mean?' said Anne.

'It killed your dogs.'

'What!' screeched Anne.

'Oh, for fuck,' growled David and stood up fast.

'Imagine this on the battlefield…' said Ben, his heart starting to race.

'Shut up,' bellowed David right into his face.

'It killed Dipsy and Widdle? How, why didn't you tell me?' and Anne grabbed David's shoulder and tried to pull him round to face her.

'Shut. Up,' he shouted and pushed her.

And she stepped backwards and she slipped and for a

second or two her arms made windmills as you do when you're trying to keep your balance but the windmills weren't big enough or fast enough or something because quite slowly she began to step backward and the ground that she meant to step back on to wasn't there. She went to put her foot on the very edge of the bank and missed. Took a step into space. Made a little squeaky noise and then fell, her skirt flapping up over her legs.

She fell into the vine.

And she screamed.

She crashed through the tight mat of tendrils and stems and runners and the vine seemed to wrap itself around her, around her bare legs and her bare arms, around her throat and over her face. It didn't, of course. The vine didn't move unless she moved it but it did seem as if it was attacking her. It did seem to be hell bent on strangling her.

And that's why Ben screamed. High and loud, like a girl.

'Fuck!' bawled David, and he stepped down the bank to try and take Anne's hand. She was thrashing and twisting and turning. She arched her back as if she was being electrocuted. She shrieked as if she was being burned. Where the vine touched her bare skin a welt came up, red and angry, as if she had been whipped.

Ben sank down, knees bent and arms tucked close to his chest in a foetal position but still on his feet. He whimpered. In his head he could hear the zip and twang of 7.62mm rounds, the muffled crump of an IED. He could hear his men screaming. He could hear Anne screaming. He joined in. David was saying something but Ben didn't know what. He seemed to want to shake Ben's hand, at least he was reaching out for him. Why? Behind David,

Anne emerged from the vine holding tight to his other hand. But was it Anne? One side of her face had ballooned like a tomato, her arms were lashed raw with reddened stripes, her jaw sagged open and one eye was closed.

David reached out again but Ben heard an old voice in his head. 'Fall back. Fall back,' it shouted and so Ben turned and ran.

·

The computer wasn't turned on. The stove wasn't lit.

Ben lay on the floor of the caravan in a foetal position wrapped in a dirty blanket and a clean sheet.

Inside his head, his thoughts were the silver spheres in a pinball machine. Each one bounced off a flipper and caromed off the back wall; they smashed into each other and fell down holes and lit up flashing warning signs and hi-scores. The noise they made was deafening. There was no pattern to them and no escape. Ben mewled to himself as he lay on the floor, clinging on. He thought of Anne screaming and David shouting at him and the blood pounding in his head as he ran back towards the van, as he ran for the Humvee and safety. He felt the sun of Helmand on his back even as he remembered running through the garden. Every thought was worse than the one before. They piled up in his head like marbles in a jar, hard and glittering.

Ben watched a patch of sunlight on the caravan floor. It was getting closer to his outstretched hand. He didn't move and yet it came towards him. It became important to Ben. It was light and warmth and it was moving slowly nearer. It reached out for him. It will take my hand and make me better, he thought. Oh, God, may that be true, thought Ben. Please may it be true.

And he hears Anne screaming, but when the light touches him and he holds its warmth in his hand, her screaming fades and he falls into a sleep.

And then he wakes.

There is silence in his head and he knows he must have slept because before he was awake he was not awake, but how long he was in that state for he has absolutely no idea. He aches from sleeping on the wooden floor. His mouth is dry and bitter tasting.

He puts the moka pot on the gas ring and waits for it to hiss.

He feels that every time he blinks he is taking a photograph of the world so that, if it should ever go away, he would have something to remember it by.

And later.

Later Ben is drinking coffee outside. His thoughts have stopped ricocheting off each other and have lined up into some sort of logical abacus.

He can't call the police because of the weed. A container full of cannabis that he has no intention of getting rid of or of getting found.

But the other weed, that nasty dangerous vine, that needs to be dealt with. It seems to Ben that what has happened here, has happened in China. It has escaped into the environment and God alone knows what happens then. Invasive species have a habit of taking over, and that's when they are nature's creation, if this stuff is engineered and weaponised then who knows what it might do.

Ben walks around his clearing, kicking disconsolately at the thick carpet of beech leaves. And behind the container he comes across the black plastic plant pot that contained his cutting of the vine.

And it is dead.

For a moment, Ben can't assimilate what he is looking at. From all his experiences over the last few months it simply doesn't make sense. The vine doesn't die. But here it is, dead.

'You are shitting me,' says Ben to the silent wood.

The vine obviously tried to live, tried to invade this space. Runners and tendrils spread out from the pot but they now lie lifeless and mouldering on the ground.

'What the fuck did that?'

He taps the pot with his foot. It barely moves. The vine has put root down through the drainage holes in the bottom of the plant pot so it didn't starve and it didn't die of thirst. Gingerly he touches one of the runners. It doesn't sting him.

'What, what, what, what?' he mutters.

And then he looks around. Hardly anything grew on the forest floor beneath the beech trees. No bramble and no bracken. Not much at all. And Ben remembers that his gaffer used to say that beech trees poisoned the ground beneath them so that there was less competition for water and food.

'Perhaps they do,' said Ben to himself, rubbing his beard. 'Perhaps they do.'

An hour later Ben was in his van bouncing down the lane toward Little Pendene.

A quarter of a mile from the property, Ben saw the familiar pattern of red stems and grey leaves in a clump on the roadside verge. How had it gotten there? Seeds eaten by a bird? Some stem or root carried out on a car tyre or the sole of a boot? Like insurgents spreading out into the province, they need to be stopped. It needs to be stopped, thought Ben in the jangle of his mind.

When he got to the gates at Little Pendene he found they were closed and padlocked shut. Even from the road he could see that the vine had started to climb over the stables and even the house itself. He stopped the van in the lane and scrambled over the gate.

'Dave,' he shouted. 'Anne. David. David. Are you here?' He saw movement through the kitchen window and a moment or so later the porch door opened and David stepped out. He was wearing chest-high waders and carrying a shotgun. He was clearly drunk.

'She's fuckin' dead yer know,' he slurred. 'Takes some doing, don't it? To get killed by a fuckin' plant.' He swayed and put his hand against the doorframe to hold himself up.

'David,' said Ben.

'Or do you think I killed her? Pushed her, I s'pose.' He sighed. 'Can't stand a woman's noise. Know what I mean? All that noise they make,' and he shook his head in exasperation at his dead wife.

'David, put the gun down, will you?'

'Died about an hour after you'd gone. She just stopped breathing. Well, it was a bit more than that. Didn't look easy for her, to be fair.'

Ben put his hands together as if in prayer. 'Please put the gun down,' he said again. 'I know how to kill it.'

'She's dead, mate. Can't kill her any more than that. She's in the front room.' Tears began to run down David's cheeks. 'I couldn't get her upstairs. She's lying on the carpet in the front room.'

Ben took a tentative step towards David. 'Put it down',

he said. 'Please, mate. Please.'

'I'd feel better if she was upstairs, I think. How strange is that?' David's eyes half-closed and he swayed unsteadily. He used the shotgun as a stick, barrels first onto the pavers just outside the door.

'That's it,' said Ben. 'Now put it down. It'll be OK. It'll all be OK.'

David's eyes opened slowly.

'No,' he said. 'No. I need to do the…' he sighed. 'I need to do it.'

Slowly, moving like a dancer underwater, David brought the barrels up until they rested on his shoulder. He tried to get the muzzles beneath his jaw but having his other hand inside the trigger guard meant that he couldn't quite do it. He frowned, like it was a trivial but perplexing problem.

'David, don't,' said Ben in a throaty voice and the glass jar in his head that contained all the beautiful marbles of his thoughts shattered and they spun a thousand fragments of colour through his mind.

David lowered the shotgun to see if he could imagine some other way of holding it in the position that he wanted but, unfortunately, it was pointing at Ben when his finger tightened on the trigger.

02.12.2018

AFTERWORD

HELLO.

If I look back at the creative world that I grew up in, it's no surprise that I have chosen to write short fiction; short stories as I used to call them.

My creative career began in advertising in the 1980s and advertising had very strict rules about length and size when it came to ideas and the writing of them. If you were writing a press ad then the headline really needed to be less than 13 words long. For a poster you had to try and get your thinking into 9 words or fewer. Radio and TV were even stricter disciplines. 30 seconds. That's the amount of time you had. Sure, some commercials ran to 60 seconds but they were fairly few and far between when I first put pen to script paper.

So I grew up to be rather sensitive to the issue of size and length.

Back then we would sit around the table or stand at the bar and fantasise about writing the great British novel or the perfect English screenplay. Looking back on it, the thing that appealed most was the size and scope and sheer bloody scale of the thing. We wanted to write an epic. Our imaginations would reign supreme if only they had sufficient space in which to soar.

But that, of course, is nonsense.

Creativity is a playful child and what it craves most of all is a safe and secure playpen. 'Do whatever you want, but do it in this space here. Within these walls, wrapped in these warm arms, you are safe to play and explore as you will.'

So, I like to think, my imagination flourished. Certainly, working in the business, I met and collaborated with world-class artists and photographers, illustrators and film directors. The people I shared an office with were some of the brightest and most beautiful creative minds you might ever wish to meet. We lived in a world where nothing was impossible and that industry led me to travel the world – very often to the parts least travelled – and ultimately to leave London and live and work in Africa and Asia.

The clock ticked and the clock tocked and by 2017 I had left the advertising business and was living in Cornwall, and that urge to write fiction surfaced once again.

But I was living in a different world. Thanks to the web, creativity could be the size and shape and length it needed to be rather than how a publisher or broadcaster wanted it to be. Box sets and eBooks had broken all the rules and shattered my old playpen's walls but that felt OK. Actually, it felt great.

I had a head-full of ideas and a life-full of experiences and now was the time to spin them together into tales. So I did.

So why SILVERBACK?

I have always been a fan of fantasy and sci-fi, not so

much because of the cloaks and assassins and spaceships but because they are spaces where ideas and concepts can be explored without being tied down directly to the world as it actually is.

I wanted to write about things that mattered to me; about ecology, about Alzheimer's, about run-away technology and urban decay, but I wanted to do it in a way that wasn't 'preachy' or trying to send a message. I suppose, without really realising it, I was falling back on my old advertising tools. Analogies were always popular as was the theory that if you wanted people to listen to what you had to say than it was a good idea to make it entertaining and interesting. You had to make it worth their while. Well, I've tried to do that. I have a love of the language and I hope that I've used it in a surprising way – and never an annoying one.

Some of the stories stand alone and some are first glimpses of new worlds that I intend to go back and investigate further. I feel as if I have stepped out of a boat onto a distant shore and put my flag in the ground, laying claim to the place.

And that's something akin to how I feel about all my writing. It's all a voyage of discovery. I don't know exactly what I'm going to find or how the tale will end. I just start somewhere that seems it might be interesting and root around, see what there is to dig up. And I admit, that sometimes means that stories have to be abandoned, pushed into a bit of unused computer memory and locked there in the dark. But those I will go back to. Perhaps a little bit later down this journey I will have picked up the key that unlocks the truth they were trying to tell.

So what can I tell you about the stories in SILVERBACK?

HIGHTIDE

'The end of the world is nigh!'

I have been hearing this my entire life, from Nostradamus to the Millennium Bug, from planet-wide plagues to global warming. Perhaps this last one, this climate change, will in fact kill us all? If that's true, we're doing exceedingly little to solve the problem and perhaps that's partly because we think we'll be among the survivors and let's be honest, to be one of the few that survives the end of the world; that would be pretty cool.

The rise in sea level would be like a biblical flood and floating on the sparkling waters, Ernie and Friday wrestle with the slippery fish that is religion and belief.

SUSTAINABLE HEAT

'Write about what you know,' isn't that what they say?

When I first settled in Cornwall I worked as a gardener; sometimes designing new ones and sometimes maintaining the old. In those years I don't think that I dug up many thrilling stories about fuchsia or lawn maintenance or when to prune flowering currants but I did meet some fascinating people; people who sparked an idea, people who drove a story.

I was very fond of the gentleman who inspired this story, but I was pretty much in my own on that.

"These are things that you should know about Barnaby Abbott. He believes in God and he's as tight-

*fisted as the very devil. Barnaby is 87 and has the face of
a wax death mask left near a warm fire."*

BRAMBLE

This is a modern-day story wearing old clothes. It's a world
of chavs and gangbangers dressed in furs and leather and
carrying swords.

In Bramble's world, council estates are stands of tree-
houses that are fifteen stories high. Drugs are expensive
and sex is, usually, free. Violence and death are just a part
of life.

It all came from a single image that just popped into my
head – as they do from time to time. That picture of urban
high-rise translated into tree houses. 'Ooh,' I thought.
'What sort of people would live there?'

Bramble lives in a world destined for more exploration.

THE SPIRE

I lived in Johannesburg for a time and there is a skyscraper
there called Ponte City. Built in 1975 it has been derelict
for many years, the tallest urban slum in Africa. The idea
of it fascinated me so I raised it up to a kilometre in height
and set it in a post-apocalypse world.

And that was my stage set. It became the analogy for
a world gone badly wrong; a world populated by the
ultra-rich and the very poor, David the billionaire in his
silk pyjamas; Zac, Margi and ninety-seven others in their
threadbare clothes. Somehow, they will all have to find a
way to live together.

THE INCIDENT ON THE B4271 (OR WHEN WORLD'S COLIDE)

This was where it began, I suppose. This was a story I told myself on a holiday in Wales and when I got back home I wrote it down and showed it to a friend.

This was the first 'short story'; before this one I thought that you spelt 'good' with an L, an O an N and a G. But this one taught me to love those little captured moments, the whiff of an atmosphere and just the hint of a bigger idea.

READY OR NOT

If someone knows your real name, that gives them power over you. People have believed that for thousands of years.

What if a man was keen to keep his identity a secret for reasons that were very twenty-first century? What if he went back into a low-tech past to achieve that?

And what if the same problem was waiting for him there?

It was an idea that came to me as I was walking the cliffs near where I live. An old belief translated into the now, an ancient version of a modern peculiarity. 'Hide and seek.' 'Here I come ready or not.' The hunter and the prey is the game that prepares us for almost every fear we will ever have.

MEMORIA

I love the idea of memory palaces. They are a testament to a life and take a lifetime to build but what might happen when decay sets in?

We dread dementia and memory loss and rightly so, but might it not be also somehow beautiful, like discovering an overgrown temple in the jungle or a ruined mausoleum on a sun-baked hill?

I think that age is one of the themes that run through these stories. We will all get old, if we are lucky enough not to die, so we should explore what changes age brings and become familiar with them, maybe even appreciate them, perhaps even see a form of beauty there.

19:84

Spoof. Homage. Rip off.

If you like reading then there are bound to be times that you want to write about what you have read. This is one such.

Nineteen eighty-four by George Orwell is beyond a classic, it's an icon. And like all icons, sometimes it needs to be mocked. I'm sure George wouldn't mind.

Other threads got spun into the weave to make the picture. The simple thought that 1984 can become another sort of time, but one which doesn't and can't exist, but hey, we live in a post-truth world where information and disinformation are equally valid and spread by the tentacles of social media so perhaps it's wrong to deny 19:84 its place on the clock and…

Well, we live in a nu-speak world, don't we?

NAMES IN THE SAND

Sometimes things are washed up on a beach and sometimes they are washed away. A beach is constantly impermanent, becoming more one thing and then another as time and tide shift. A beach is sea you can walk on, land that drowns.

I live just two miles inland from one of the most stunning beaches in England. One misty morning I walked through the mizzle and haze out onto miles of glass-smooth sand. I looked up to discover that the world had completely disappeared; up and down, left and right and front to back, all I could see was a featureless, pewter-grey sheen.

This story was written into my head right then and there.

IF A TREE FALLS

This story began with me having fun with a 'fake-news' Facebook post, a sort of Orson Wells, War of the Worlds 'live' on radio thing. I posted some updates on social media that were written as if this story was true and I was experiencing it. That got quite a good reaction on social media so I expanded a few hundred words to a few thousand and here we are.

There was another strand to it as well. 'Call yourself an eco-warrior? How hard would you fight? What would you risk losing?'

Yes, it's easy to see that mankind has had a bad effect on our planet's ecosystem but take that to its logical conclusion. If there were a way to wipe out all that damage but possibly all of human history too, would you push that button?

WEED

This is probably the biggest blend of fact and fiction that I've written to date. I worked in this garden. I knew a couple very similar to this couple, but no one died and the continued existence of all human life on the surface of the planet was never threatened, at least not as far as I noticed.

As for the idea, well, if you've ever been locked in a struggle with weeds and brambles you will know how it can come to take over your whole life.

Gardens are good places to think about things; gardening is a good pastime – or even job – for a writer. The story touches on our arrogant manipulation of nature when we have little or no real idea of the consequences. It touches on PTSD, which I know rather more about than I would wish. Perhaps mostly what it's about is the awkward nature of human nature.

Thank you.

Thank you for reading this and thank you for reading these stories.

I hope that you enjoyed them. The coffee maker is going on now. A nice, gutsy espresso, then I think I'll brew up some more tales for you.

Love to all xx xx